George MacDonald
The Peasant Girl's Dream

George MacDonald
The Peasant Girl's Dream

Michael R. Phillips, Editor

BETHANY HOUSE PUBLISHERS
MINNEAPOLIS, MINNESOTA 55438
A Division of Bethany Fellowship, Inc.

Cover illustration by Dan Thornberg,
Bethany House Publishers staff artist.

Originally published in 1893 as HEATHER AND SNOW
by Chaddo & Windus, London.

Published by Bethany House Publishers
A Division of Bethany Fellowship, Inc.
6820 Auto Club Road, Minneapolis, Minnesota 55438

Printed in the United States of America

Library of Congress Cataloging-in-Publication Data

MacDonald, George, 1824–1905.
   [Heather and snow]
   The peasant girl's dream / George MacDonald ; Michael R. Phillips, editor.
     p.   cm.
   Originally published as: Heather and snow in 1893 by Chaddo & Windus,
London.

I. Phillips, Michael R., 1946–   . II. Title.
PR4967.H4   1989
823'.8—dc19   88–33336
ISBN 1-55661-023-8   CIP

Scottish Fiction by George MacDonald
retold for today's reader by Michael Phillips

The two-volume story of Malcolm:
The Fisherman's Lady
The Marquis' Secret

Companion stories of Gibbie and his friend Donal:
The Baronet's Song
The Shepherd's Castle

Companion stories of Hugh Sutherland and Robert Falconer:
The Tutor's First Love
The Musician's Quest

Companion stories of Thomas Wingfold:
The Curate's Awakening
The Lady's Confession
The Baron's Apprenticeship

Stories that stand alone:
A Daughter's Devotion
The Gentlewoman's Choice
The Highlander's Last Song
The Laird's Inheritance
The Maiden's Bequest
The Minister's Restoration
The Peasant Girl's Dream

The George MacDonald Collector's Library—
beautifully bound hardcover editions:
The Fisherman's Lady
The Marquis' Secret

A New Biography of George MacDonald
by Michael Phillips

George MacDonald: Scotland's Beloved Storyteller

Contents

Introduction

The fourth from the last book written by George MacDonald in his long career was entitled *Heather and Snow*. It was published in 1893 and is not particularly distinguished among MacDonald's lengthy list of more notable titles, except for the fact that in *Heather and Snow*, MacDonald returned once again to that setting he always loved so well—the Scottish highlands near his place of birth, the country cottage, the large-hearted peasantry, the fierce highland weather, and the bonds of simple relationships. *Heather and Snow*, here retitled *The Peasant Girl's Dream* for the Bethany House reprint series, becomes then something of a composite of those peculiarly "Scottish" features MacDonald loved to bring into his books whenever he had the opportunity. For MacDonald was indeed Scotland's storyteller.

The mere mention of a peat fire carries one's imagination beyond the town into the little crofting cottages of thatched roof and dirt floor, from which could be seen the friendly curl of smoke rising slowly into the sky, yielding the sweet aroma of the burning peat within. . . .

Much in George MacDonald's writings recalls to mind the simple ways of these unpretentious people and their agrarian lifestyle. To understand the man we must also know the world of George MacDonald's nurture and growth—for the land was always feeding him, influencing him. In his novels, his poetry, and his fairy tales, we see themes constantly repeated that hearken back to his own boyhood in Huntly—castles, noble families, cobblestone village streets, warm summers, icy rivers, golden-brown burns and rivers, fields of ripening grain, heather moors, poverty and wealth, peat fires, and homely meals of

9

boiled potatoes and oatcakes. His boyhood imagination saw beyond the surface appearance of these influences and gave birth to a romantic vision of a time now past. . . . A good deal from his writings and much of what he was as a man sprang from this source.

C. Edward Troup, George MacDonald's cousin, wrote: "I do not know of any other writer the scenes of whose boyhood were so deeply impressed on him and are so closely associated with his best work. In his English novels he wrote, of course, of English country scenes, but never, I think, with the same love as of Scotland; and when he writes of Scotland, one almost always feels it is Aberdeenshire."[1]

Heather and Snow depicts the low highlands of the Grampian Mountains west of Aberdeen at its most vivid, set in the same region as *Salted with Fire* (*The Minister's Restoration* in the Bethany House series) and tells a humble story of the enduring quality of love—between a man and his friend, between parents and children, between brother and sister, between man and woman, and between a simple-minded boy and his God. What you read here may not turn your world upside-down with startling revelations. This is a quiet story, to be savored as its influences and relationships and perspectives soak gently into your spirit.

In the editing of *A Peasant Girl's Dream*, I have left approximately a quarter of the Scot's dialect. If it is difficult for you at first, stick with it. You will quickly grow accustomed to its flavor; and when you do, you will find your experience enriched as a result.

May the Lord bless you as you enjoy this thoroughly Scottish tale that follows.

Michael Phillips

---

[1]Michael Phillips, *George MacDonald: Scotland's Beloved Storyteller* (Minneapolis, Minn.: Bethany House Publishers, 1987), pp. 44–46.

1 / The Race

The land was not pretty, unless you knew where to look for its beauty. Neither was it friendly, unless you lived upon it long enough to make it a friend. In truth, it was a rugged place—sparse of grass, sparser still of trees, and almost devoid of humankind. Unless, that is, you knew where to find them.

The people of this region were not unlike the land, which grew more of the wiry shrub called heather than anything. A sinewy and hardy lot they were, contented mostly to carve out what existence they could from the land that was the only home they had ever known. The border region of the eastern Scottish highlands was not so stark a place as the more mountainous territory farther west and farther north. Yet it yielded its bounty grudgingly, and every winter seemed determined to wipe all trace of living things from its face. Somehow, nevertheless, the consciousness of nature managed to sleep under the blankets of snow, held in a suspended frozen warmth against the icy blasts sweeping down from the north, until spring sent forth its miracle from unknown depths, as it had thousands of times before, and life came once more to the land.

Both peasants and landowners found a way to coexist in a harmony of want, the latter hardly better off than the former in these years of the nineteenth century. In the region near the small village of Tiltowie, two men—friends who had grown up together, then served as comrades in India in the fifties—had each farmed the land all their adult lives in the relation of landlord and tenant.

One was now gone, but his memory lived on in his companion as the years passed. It now remained for their children to carry on the love that had bound the hearts of those two men together, and throughout their childhood it seemed that the bonds that had ignored social distinctions between the elders would indeed be strong enough in the children to accomplish the same. For the daughter of the one loved the son of the other, first with the love of a true friend, then with the love of One greater whom she grew to know. But her devotion would be sorely tested through the son's prodigal years of foolish self-indulgence, as would her father's dedication to serve the son and family of his departed comrade.

As yet, however, neither father nor daughter could foresee the path the boy was determined to walk before coming to himself. He was still a lad, though growing rapidly into something more, and only hints were yet visible of the demon of self that was rising within his heart. Unknown to him, it was this lurking evil spirit in his own soul that would become the fiercest enemy with which he would be called upon to do battle.

At the time, however, all he could envision in his youthful fancy was leading the charge against more temporal foes. And it was just such fancies he was now speaking of to the daughter of his father's truest friend.

Upon neighboring stones, held fast to the earth like two islands of an archipelago in an ocean of heather, sat this boy and this girl. The girl was knitting, or, as she would have called it, weaving a stocking, and the boy was talking very excitedly in an animated voice, with his eyes fixed on her face. He had great fluency, and could have talked just as fast in good English as in the dialect in which he was now pouring out his ambitions—the broad Saxon of Aberdeen. They were both about fifteen.

The boy was telling the girl that he meant to be a soldier like his father, and quite as good a one as he too. He knew so little of himself or the world, and was so moved by the results he anticipated without regard for the actions it would take on his part to reach them that he saw success as already his, and a grateful country at his feet. His inspiration was so purely self-motivated ambition that even if he were to achieve much for his country, Kirsty doubted that she would owe him much gratitude.

"I'll no hae the world make lightly o' me!" he said.

"Maybe the world winna trouble itsel' aboot ye sae muckle as to think o' ye at all!" returned his companion quietly.

"What for are ye scoffin' at me?" retorted the boy, rising and looking down on her in displeasure. "A body canna let his thoughts go but ye're doon upon them like birds upon corn!"

"I wouldna be scoffin' at ye, Francie, but that I care too muckle aboot ye to let ye think I hold the same opinion o' ye that ye hae o' yersel'," answered the girl, who went on with her knitting as she spoke.

"Ye'll never believe a body!" he rejoined, and turned half away. "I canna think what makes me keep comin' to see ye! Ye haena one good word to gie a body!"

"It's none ye'll get frae me, the way ye're gaein, Francie! Ye think a heap too muckle o' yersel'. What ye expect may someday all come true, but ye hae given naebody a right to expect it along wi' ye; and I canna think, if ye were fair to yersel', that ye would count yersel' one it was to be expected o'."

"I tauld ye sae, Kirsty! Ye never lay any weight upon what a body says!"

"That depends upon the body. Did ye never hear Mr. Craig point oot the difference atween believin' a body and believin' *in* a body, Francie?"

"No—and I dinna care."

"I wouldna like ye to gang away thinkin' I doobted yer word, Francie. I believe anything ye tell me, as far as I think ye ken, but maybe no sae far as *ye* think ye ken. I believe ye, but I confess I dinna believe *in* ye—yet. What hae ye ever done to gie a body any right to believe in ye? Ye're a good rider, and a good shot for a laddie, and ye run middlin' fast—I canna say like a deer, for I reckon I could lick ye mysel'! But—"

"Who's braggin' noo, Kirsty?" cried the boy, with a touch of ill-humored triumph.

"Me," answered Kirsty; "—and I'll do what I brag o'!" she added, throwing her stocking on the patch of green sward near the stone and jumping to her feet with a laugh. "Is it to be uphill or along the flat?"

They were near the foot of a hill where the heather flowed to the top, but along whose base, between the heather and the bog-land below, lay an irregular belt of moss and grass, pretty much clear of stones. The boy did not seem eager to accept the challenge.

"There's nae good in lickin' a lassie!" he said with a shrug.

"There might be good in tryin' to do it, though—especially if ye were licked at it!" returned the girl.

"What good can there be in a body bein' licked at anything?"

"The good o' haein' that body's pride taken doon a wee."

"I'm no sae sure o' the good o' that! It would only keep ye frae tryin' again."

"There!—that's jist what yer pride does to ye, Francie! Ye must aye be first, or ye'll no try! Ye'll never do naethin' for fear o' no bein' able to believe ye could do it better than any other body! Ye dinna want to find oot that ye're naebody in particular. It's a sore pity ye winna hae yer pride taken doon. Ye would be much better wi' aboot three parts less o' it. Come, I'm ready for ye! Never mind that I'm a lassie. Naebody will ken!"

"Ye hae nae shoes," objected the boy.

"Ye can pull off yer own."

"My feet's no sae hard as yers!"

"Weel, I'll put mine on. They're here, sich as they are. Ye see, I need them gaein through the heather; that's some sore upon the feet! Straight up the hill through the heather, and I'll put my shoes on!"

"I'm no sae good uphill."

"See there noo, Francie! Ye take yersel' for so courteous and honorable and generous and knightly and all that—oh, I ken all aboot it, and it's all very weel sae far as it goes. But what the better are ye for it, when all the time ye winna even run up the hill cause a body's a girl. Ye must hae every advantage, or ye winna gie her a chance o' lickin' ye. Here! I'll put on my shoes and run ye along the flat ground! My shoes is twice the weight o' yers, and they dinna fit me.''

The boy did not care to go on refusing. He feared what Kirsty would say next. But he relished nothing at all in the challenge. It was not fit for a man to run races with a girl. There was nothing to be won by a victory over her, and in his heart he was not at all sure of beating Kirsty. She had always beaten him when they were children. Since then they had been at the parish school together, but there public opinion kept the boys and girls to their own special activities. Now Kirsty had left school, and Francis was going to the grammar school at the county town in preparation for college.

All the common sense was on the side of the girl, and she had been doing her best to make the boy more practical—hitherto without much success, although he was by no means a bad sort of fellow. He had not yet passed the stage—some appear never to pass it in this world—in which an admirer feels himself in the same category with his hero. Many are content with themselves because they side with those whose ways they do not endeavor to follow. Such are most who call themselves Christians. If men admired themselves for what they did, their conceit would be greatly moderated.

Kirsty put on her heavy hobnailed shoes—much too large for her, having been made for her brother—stood up erect, put her elbows back, and said, "I'll gie ye a head start to the stane wi' the heather growin' oot o' the top o' it."

"Na, na. I'll hae none o' that!" answered Francis. "Fair play to a'!"

"Ye'd better take it!"

"Off wi' ye, or I winna run at a'!" cried the boy—and away they went.

Kirsty contrived that he should yet have a little best of her at the beginning—how much from generosity and how much from determination that there should be nothing doubtful in the result, I cannot say—and for a good many yards he kept in the lead. But if the boy, who ran well, had looked back, he might have seen that the girl was not doing her best. Presently she quickened her pace and lessened the distance between them. When he became aware of her approach, the boy quickened his steps too, and for a time there was little change in their relative position. Then she sped up again—with an ease which made her seem capable of going on to accelerate indefinitely—and rapidly overtook him. She passed him swiftly and did not once look around or slow down until she had left him far behind and put a shoulder of the hill between them.

The moment she passed him, the boy flung himself on the ground and lay. The girl had felt certain he would do so, and fancied she heard him flop among the heather. But she could not be sure, for her blood was making tunes in her head, and the wind was blowing in and out of her ears with a pleasant but loud accompaniment. When she knew he could see her no longer, she also stopped and threw herself down for a few minutes, wondering whether she should leave him or walk back at her leisure. She came to the conclusion that it would be kinder to allow him to get over his discomfort in private. She rose, therefore, and went straight up the hill.

About halfway to the summit, she climbed a rock as if she were a goat, and looked all around her. Then she uttered a shrill, peculiar cry, and listened. No answer came. Getting down as easily as she had gotten up, she walked along the side of the hill, making her way nearly parallel with their recent race course, so that she passed considerably above the spot where her defeated rival still lay, and descended at length into a little hollow not far from where she and Francis had been sitting.

In this hollow, which was covered with short, sweet grass, stood a very small hut, built of turf from the peat moss fields below, and roofed with sods on which the heather still stuck, if indeed some of it was not still growing. It was therefore so similar to the color of the ground all about it that it scarcely caught the eye. Its walls and its roof were so thick that, small as it looked, it was smaller inside, while outside it could not have measured more than ten feet in length, eight in width, and seven in height. Kirsty and her brother, Steenie, not without help from Francis Gordon, had built it for themselves two years before. Their father knew nothing of the scheme until one day, proud of their success, Steenie wanted him to see their handiwork. His father was so much pleased with it that he made them a door, on which he put a lock.

"For though this isna the kind o' place to draw crook-fingered gentry," he said, "some gangrel body might creep in and make his bed in it, and that lock'll be enough to hold him oot, I'm thinkin'."

He also cut a hole through the wall for them, and fitted it with a window that opened and shut, which was more than could be said of every window at their farmhouse.

Into this nest Kirsty now went, and remained there until it began to grow dark. She had hoped to find her brother waiting for her. But although she was disappointed, she chose to continue there until Francis Gordon was well on his way to the castle, when she crept out and ran to recover her stocking.

When she got home, she found Steenie engrossed in a young horse their father had just bought. She would have liked to mount him at once, for she would ride any kind of animal that could carry her. But as he had never yet had anyone on his back, her father would not let her.

2 / Mother and Son_____

Francis lay for some time on the heather, thinking Kirsty was sure to come back to him, but half-wishing she would not. At length he rose to see whether she was on the way; but no one was in sight. The place suddenly became dreadful with loneliness, as it must indeed have looked to anyone not at peace with solitude. Having sent several ringing shouts after Kirsty, with no answer, he turned, and in the descending light of an autumn afternoon, set out on the rather long walk to his home, which was the wearier because he had nothing pleasant at hand to think about.

He had about a three-mile walk, and along the way had to pass the farm where Kirsty lived. At length he came to the ancient, turreted house on the top of a low hill, where his mother sat expecting him, ready to tyrannize over him as usual—and none-theless ready since he was going to leave her within a week.

"Where have you been all day?" she said.

"I have been on a long walk," he answered.

"You've been to Corbyknowe!" she returned. "I know it by your eyes! I know by the very color of them you're going to deceive me! Now don't tell me you haven't been there. I won't believe you!"

"I haven't been near the place, Mother," said Francis. But as he said it his face glowed with a heat that did not come from the fire. He was not naturally an untruthful boy, and what he said was technically correct, for he had passed the house half a mile away. But his words gave, and were intended to give the impression that he had not been that day with any of the people of Corbyknowe.

18

His mother objected to his visiting the farmer, but he knew instinctively that she would have objected yet more to his spending half the day with Kirsty, whom she never mentioned. Little as she loved her son, Mrs. Gordon would have scorned to suspect him of preferring the society of such a girl to her own. In truth, however, there were very few of his acquaintances whose company Francis would not have chosen rather than his mother's— except indeed if he was ill, when she was generally very good to him.

"Well, this once I shall believe you," she answered, "and I am glad to be able to. It is a painful thought to me, Frank, that a son of mine should feel the smallest attraction to low company. I have told you twenty times that the man was nothing but a private in your father's regiment."

"He was my father's friend," answered the boy.

"He tells you so, I do not doubt," returned the mother. "He was not likely to leave that moldy stone unturned!"

The mother sat, and the son stood before her, in a drawing room whose furniture of a hundred years old must once have looked very modern and new-fangled under windows so narrow and high up, and within walls so thick: without a fire it was always cold. The carpet was very dingy and the mirrors were spotted. But the poverty of the room was the respectable poverty of age. A good fire of mingled peat and coal burned brightly in the barrel-fronted steel grate, and shone red in the brass fender. The face, too, of the boy looked very red in the glow, but its color came more from within than without. He cherished the memory of his father, and did not love his mother more than a little.

"He has told me more about my father than you ever did, Mother," he answered.

"Well he may have!" she returned. "Your father was not a young man when I married him, and they had been through I don't know how many campaigns together."

"And you say he was not my father's friend!"

"Not his *friend*, Frank; his servant—what do they call

them?—his orderly, I daresay. Certainly not his friend."

"Any man may be another's friend."

"Not in the way you mean. Not that his son should go and see him every other day. A dog may be a man's good friend, and so was Sergeant Barclay your father's—a very good friend that way, I don't doubt."

"You said he was but a private, and now you call him Sergeant Barclay."

"What's the difference?"

"To be made a sergeant shows that he was not a common man. If he had been, he would not have been set over others."

"Of course he was then, and is now, a very respectable man. If he were not, I should never have let you go to see him at all. But you must learn to behave like the gentleman you are, and that you never will while you frequent the company of your inferiors. Your manners are already almost ruined—fit for nothing but a farmhouse! There you are, standing on the side of your foot again!—Old Barclay, I daresay, tells you no end of stories about your mother!"

"He always asks about you, Mother, and then never mentions you again."

She knew perfectly that the boy spoke the truth.

"Don't let me hear of your being there again before you go to school," she said with derision. "By the time you come home next year, I trust your tastes will have improved. Go and make yourself tidy for dinner. A soldier's son must always tend to his dress."

Francis went to his room. It was impossible for him to have told his mother that he had been with Kirsty Barclay, that he had run a race with her, and that she had left him alone at the foot of the Horn. No one who knew his mother's stormy and unreasoning temper would have wondered why he could not be open with her. But the pitiful boy, who did not like lying, actually congratulated himself that he had gotten through without telling a downright falsehood. It would not have bettered matters in the least had he disclosed to her the good advice Kirsty gave him. She would only have been furious at the impudence of the hussy in talking so to *her* son.

3 / At the Foot of the Horn

The region was like a waste place in the troubled land of dreams—a spot so barren that the dreamer struggles to rouse himself from his dream, finding it too dreary to dream on. I have heard it likened to "the ill place, wi' the fire oot," but that was not quite right. There was nothing to suggest the silence of once-roaring flame, no half-molten rocks, no depths within depths blooming mystery and ancient horror. It was the more desolate that it moved no active sense of dismay.

There was a wide stretch of damp-looking level, mostly of undetermined or of a low-toned color, with here and there a black spot, or, on the border of it, the brighter green of a patch of some growing crop. Flat and wide, the eye found it difficult to rest upon it and not sweep hurriedly from border to border for lack of any object to light upon. It looked low, but indeed lay high; the bases of the hills surrounding it were far above the sea. These hills at this season of the year, appeared to make of the high valley a huge circular basin, miles in diameter, over the rim of which peered the tops and peaks of mountains more distant. Up the side of the Horn, which was the loftiest in the ring, ran a stone wall, or in the language of the country, a *dry-stane dyke*, of considerable size, climbing to the very top. There was nothing but the grouse to have rendered it worth the proprietor's while to erect such a boundary to his neighbor's property, plentiful as were the stones ready for that poorest use of any material object—division.

The farms that bordered the hollow, running each a little way up the side of the basin, were—some of them at least—as well cultivated as any in Scotland. But in that region winter claims supremacy and yields to summer so few of its rights that the place looked forbidding nearly at all times to such as do not live in it. To love it, I think one must have been born there. In the summer, it is true, it has the character of bracing, but can be such, I imagine, only to those who are pretty well braced already; the delicate of certain sorts, I think it must soon brace with the bands of death.

The region was in constant danger of famine. If the snow came but a little earlier than usual, the crops would lie green under it, and no store of grain and meal could be laid up in the cottages against the winter. Then, if the snow continued to lie deep, the difficulty of conveying even the most minimal supplies caused the dwellers there no little hardship. Of course, such dwellers are few, and the cottages to be seen were scattered about at great distances.

It was now summer, and in a month or two the landscape would look more cheerful. The heather that covered the hills would no longer be dry and brown and in places black with fire, but a blaze of red purple, a rich mantle of bloom. Even now, early in July, the sun possessed a little power. I cannot say it would have been warm had there been the least motion in the air, for seldom indeed could one there from the south grant that the wind had no keen edge to it. But on this morning there was absolute stillness, and although it was not easy for Kirsty to imagine any summer air other than warm, yet the wind's absence had not a little to do with the sense of luxurious life that now filled her heart.

She sat on her favorite grassy slope near the foot of the cone-shaped Horn, looking over the level miles before her, and knitting away at a ribbed stocking of dark blue whose toe she had nearly finished, glad in the thought, not of rest from her labor, but of beginning the yet more important fellow stocking. She had no need to look closely at her work to keep the loops right, but she was so careful and precise that if she lived to be old and blind, she would knit better then than now. It was to her the perfect glory of a summer day, and I imagine her delight in the divine luxury greater than that of many a poet dwelling in softer climates.

The spot where she sat was close by the turf hut that I have already described. At every shifting of a needle she would send a new glance all over her world, a glance to remind one somehow of the sweep of a broad ray of sunlight across earth and sea, when, on a morning of upper wind, the broken clouds take endless liberties with shadow and shine. What she saw I cannot tell; I know she saw far more than a stranger would have seen, for she knew her home.

Her eyes were probably drawn chiefly to those intense spots of life—white, opaque yet brilliant, the heads of the cotton grass here and there scattered about in thin patches on the dark ground. For nearly the whole of the level was a gigantic field of peat moss. Miles and miles of peat, differing in quality and varying in depth, lay between those hills, almost the only fuel of the region. In some spots it was very wet, water lying beneath and all through its substance. In others, dark spots, the sides of the holes out of which it had been dug, showed where it was drier. Her eyes might rest a moment also on those black spaces on the hills where the old heather had been burned that its roots might shoot afresh and feed the grouse with soft young sprouts, their chief support. They looked now like neglected spots where men cast stones and shards, but by and by they would be covered with a tenderer green than the rest of the hillside. A stranger would not see the moorland birds that Kirsty saw. He would only hear their cries, with now and then perhaps the bark of a sheep dog.

To one who does not love the region, I say, it will probably sound altogether uninteresting, even ugly. But certainly Christina Barclay did not think it such. The girl was more than well-satisfied with the world-shell in which she found herself. She was at the moment basking, both bodily and spiritually, in a full sense of the world's bliss. Her soul was bathed in its own content, calling none of its feelings to account. The sun, the air, the wide expanse, the hilltops' nearness to the heavens which yet they could not invade, the little breaths that every now and then awoke to assert their existence by immediately ceasing, doubtless also the knowledge that her stocking was nearly done, that her father and mother were but a mile or so away, that she knew where Steenie was, and that a cry would bring him to her feet—all these things each played a part in making Kirsty quiet with satisfaction. That there was, all the time, a deeper cause of her peace Kirsty knew well—the same that is the root of life itself. And if it was not at this moment or that filled with conscious gratitude, her heart was yet like a bird ever on the point of springing up to soar, and often soaring indeed. Whether it came of something special in her constitution that happiness always made her quiet, as nothing but sorrow will some, I do not presume to say. I only know that had her bliss changed suddenly to sadness, Kirsty would have been quiet still. Whatever came to Kirsty seemed right, for, there it was.

She was now a girl of sixteen. Almost a year had passed since she had last talked to Francis. The only sign she showed of interest in her person appeared in her hair and the covering of her neck. Of one of the many middle shades of brown, with a rippling tendency to curl in it, her hair was nicely parted and drawn back from her face into a net of its own color, while her neckerchief was of blue silk. It covered a very white skin, leaving bare a brown throat. She wore a blue print wrapper, not much differing from that of a peasant woman, and a blue winsey petticoat, out from under which appeared her bare feet, lovely in shape and brown of hue. Her dress was not particularly trim, and suggested neither tidiness nor disorder. The hem was in truth a little torn, but not more than what might seem admissible where the rough wear to which the garment was necessarily exposed was considered. When a little worse, it would receive proper attention and be brought back to respectability. Kirsty grudged the time spent on her clothes. She looked down on them as the moon might on the clouds around her. She made or mended them to wear, not to think about.

Her forehead was wide and rather low, with straight eyebrows. Her eyes were of a gentle hazel, not the hazel that looks black at night. Her nose was strong, a little irregular, with plenty of substance, and sensitive nostrils. A decided and well-shaped chin dominated a neck by no means slender, and seemed to assert the superiority of the face over the whole beautiful body. Its chief expression was of a strong repose—a sweet, powerful peace, requiring but occasion to pass into determination.

I wish it were possible to see the mind of a woman grow as she sits spinning or weaving: it would reveal the process next highest to creation. But the only hope of ever understanding such things lies in growing oneself. There is the still growth of the moonlit night of reverie. Cloudy, with wind and a little rain, comes the morning of thought when the mind grows faster and the heart more slowly. Then wakes the storm in the forest of the human soul when it enlarges itself by great bursts of vision and leaps of understanding and resolve. Then floats up the mystic twilight eagerness, when the soul is driven toward that which is before, grasping at it with all the hunger of the new birth. The story of God's universe lies in the growth of the individual soul. Kirsty's growth had been as yet quiet and steady.

Once more as she shifted her needle, her glance went flitting over the waste before her. This time there was more life in sight. Far away Kirsty could see something of the nature of a man upon a horse. To say how far away would have been as difficult for one unused to the flat moor as for a landsman to reckon distances at sea. Most people of the place would not have seen anything at all. At length, after she had looked many times, she could clearly distinguish a youth on a strong, handsome hill pony. There was no longer the slightest doubt who it was.

He came steadily over the dark surface of the moor, and it was clear that his pony must know the nature of the ground well; for as he went, now he galloped along as fast as he could go, now made a succession of short jumps, and now half halted, and began slowly picking his way.

Gordon had seen her on the hillside, probably long before she saw him, and had been coming toward her in as straight a line as the ground would permit. Before long he was out of the boggy level and ascending the slope of the hill-foot to where she sat. When he was within about twenty yards of her, she gave him a little nod. He held on till within a few feet of her, then pulled up and threw himself from the pony's back. The creature stood a minute panting, covered with foam, then fell to work on the short grass.

Francis had grown considerably, and looked almost like a young man. He was a little older than Kirsty, but did not appear so, his expression being a great deal younger than hers. Whether self-indulgence or aspiration was to come out of his evident joy in life seemed yet undetermined. His countenance indicated nothing bad. He might well have represented one at the point before having to choose whether to go up or down hill. He was dressed a little showily in a short coat of dark tartan and a highland bonnet with a brooch and feather, and carried a lady's riding whip—his mother's no doubt. His appearance was altogether a contrast to that of the girl. She was a peasant, he a gentleman. Her bare head and yet more bare feet emphasized the contrast all the more. But which was by nature and in fact the superior, no one with the least insight could have doubted.

He stood and looked at her, but neither spoke. She cast at length a glance upward, and said, "Weel?"

For several moments Francis said nothing—indeed, seemed able to say nothing. In his face began to appear indication of growing displeasure: was this his only welcome? a single word? On her part, with complete self-possession, Kirsty sat in silence, leaving the initiative to the one who had sought the interview. At last, however, she appeared to think she must take mercy on him: how he had changed in his treatment of her!

"That's a bonny pony ye hae," she remarked, with a look at the creature.

"Ay, it is," he answered dryly.

"Whaur did ye get it?" she asked.

"My mither bought it for my homecomin'," he replied.

"She must hae a straight eye for a good beast," returned Kirsty, with a second glance at the pony.

"He's a bonny cratur, and willin'," answered the youth. "He'll run through anything—water anyway—I'm no sae sure aboot fire."

A long silence followed, this time broken by the youth.

"Winna ye gie me look nor word, and me ridin' like mad to hae a sight o' ye?" he said.

She glanced up at him.

"Weel, ye hae that!" she answered, with a smile that showed her lovely white teeth. "Ye're sae a' dressed up! What for should ye be in sich a hurry? Ye saw me jist three days ago."

"Ay, I saw ye. But I didna get a word wi' ye."

"Ye was free to say what ye liked. There was none by but my mither."

"Would ye hae me say a' things afore yer mither jist as I would to ye alone?" he asked.

"Ay, would I," she returned. "Then she would ken, wi'oot my haein' to tell her what a goose ye was."

Had he not seen the sunny smile that accompanied her words, he might well have taken offense.

Silence again fell.

"Weel, what would ye hae, Francie?" said Kirsty at length.

"I would hae ye promise to marry me, Kirsty, come the time," he answered, "and that ye ken as weel as I do mysel'."

"That's straight anyway!" rejoined Kirsty. "But ye see, Francie," she went on, "yer father, when he left ye a kind o' a legacy, as ye may call it, to mine, had no intention that *I* was to be left oot; neither had *my* father when he accepted o' it."

"I dinna understand ye one atom!"

"Hold yer tongue then and hearken," returned Kirsty. "What I'm meanin' is this: what lies to my father's hand lies to mine as weel. And I'll never hae it kenned or said that when my father pulled one way, I pulled anither.''

"Sakes, lassie! what *are* ye runnin' on aboot? Would it be pullin' against yer father to marry *me*?''

"It would be that.''

"I dinna see hoo ye can make that oot! I dinna see hoo, bein' sich a friend o' my father's, yer father should object to my father's son.''

"Eh, but laddies are gowks!'' cried Kirsty. "My father was yer father's friend for *his* sake, no for his own! He thinks o' what would be good for ye, no for himsel'.''

"Weel, but,'' persisted Gordon, "it would be more for my good nor anything else he could wish for, to hae ye for my wife!''

"A bonnie wife ye would hae, Francie Gordon, who, kennin' her father was doin' every mortal thing for the love o' his auld master and comrade, took the fine chance to make her own o' it, and kept her grip o' the lad for hersel'! Do ye think that either o' the two auld men ever want sich a thing as fatherin' both? That my father had a lass-bairn o' his own showed more than anything the trust yer father put in him! Francie, the very grave would cast me oot for shame that I' should hae once thought o' the thing. Man, it would most drive yer leddy-mither demented!''

"It's my business, Kirsty, who I marry!''

"And I hope yer grace'll alloo it's part my business who ye shall not marry—and that's me, Francie!''

Gordon sprang to his feet with such a look of anger and despair as for a moment frightened Kirsty, who was not easily frightened. She thought of the terrible bog holes on the way her lover had come, sprang also to her feet, and caught him by the arm where, his foot already in the stirrup, he stood in the act of mounting.

"Francie! Francie!'' she cried, "hearken to reason! There's no a body, man or woman, I like better than yersel'—'cept my father, o' coorse, and my mither, and my own Steenie!''

"And hoo many mair, if I had the will to hear the long Bible chapter o' them, and see mysel' comin' in at the tail o' them a'! Na, na, it's time I was home! If ye had a score o' idiot brithers,

ye would care more for every one o' them than for me! I canna
bide to think o' it!"

"It's true a' the same," returned the girl, her face, which had
been very pale, now rosy with indignation. "My Steenie's more
to me than a' the Gordons together, Bow-o-meal or Jock-and-Tam
as ye like!"

She drew back, sat down again to the stocking she was knitting
for Steenie, and left Francis to mount and ride, which he did
without another word.

"There's more nor one kind o' idiot," she said to herself,
"and Steenie's no the kind that ought to be called one. There's
more in Steenie than in six Francie Gordons!"

If ever Kirsty came to love a man, it would be nothing to her
to die for him.

But then it never would have been anything to her to die for
her father or her mother or Steenie.

Gordon galloped off at a wild pace, as if he would drive his
pony straight into the terrible moss, taking hag and well-eye as
it came. But glancing back and seeing that Kirsty was not looking
after him, he turned the creature's head in a safer direction, and
left the moss at his back.

4 / Steenie the Dog

She sat for some time at the foot of the hill, motionless as itself, except for her hands. The sun shone on in silence, and the blue butterflies that haunted the little bush of bluebells beside her made no noise. Only a stray bee, happy in the pale heat, made a little music to please itself—and perhaps the butterflies.

Kirsty had an unusual power of sitting still, even with nothing for her hands to do. On the present occasion, however, her hands and fingers went faster than usual—not entirely from eagerness to finish her stocking, but partly from her displeasure with Francie. At last she broke her worsted, drew the end of the thread through the final loop, and, drawing it, rose and scanned the side of the hill. Not far off she spied the fleecy backs of a few feeding sheep, and immediately she sent out to the still air a sweet, strong, musical cry. It was instantly responded to by a bark from somewhere up the hill. She sat down, clasped her hands over her knees, and waited.

She did not have to wait long. A sound of rushing came through the heather, and in a moment or two a fine collie, with a long, silky, wavy coat of black and brown, and one white spot on his face, shot out of the heather, sprang upon her, and, setting his paws on her shoulders, began licking her face. She threw her arms round him, and addressed him in words of fondling rebuke: "Ye ill-mannered tyke!" she said; "what right hae ye to take the place o' yer betters? Get doon wi' ye and wait. But eh, ye're a fine doggie!"

While she scolded, she let him caress her as he pleased. Presently he left her, and going a yard or two away, threw himself on the grass with such abandon as no animal but a weary dog seems capable of reaching. He had made haste to be first that he might caress her before his master came. Now he heard him close behind, and knew his opportunity was over.

Stephen came next out of the heather, creeping to Kirsty's feet on all fours. He was a gaunt, long-backed lad, who at certain seasons, undetermined, either imagined himself the animal he imitated, or had some notion of being required, or, possibly, compelled to behave like a dog. When the fit was upon him, all the day long he would speak no word even to his sister, would only bark or give a low growl like the collie. In this last he succeeded much better than in running like him, although, indeed, his arms were so long that it was comparatively easy for him to use them as forelegs. He let his head hang low as he went, throwing it up to bark, and sinking it yet lower when he growled, which was seldom, and to those that loved him indicated great trouble. He did not, like Snootie, raise himself on his hind legs to caress his sister, but gently subsided upon her feet, and there lay panting, his face to the earth and his forearms crossed beneath his nose.

Kirsty stooped and stroked and patted him as if he were the dog he seemed fain to be. Then drawing her feet from under him, she rose, went a little way up the hill to the hut, and returned presently with a basin full of rich-looking milk and a piece of thick oatcake that she had brought from home in the morning. The milk she set beside her as she resumed her seat. Then she put her feet again under the would-be dog, and proceeded to break small pieces from the oatcake and throw them to him. He sought every piece eagerly as it fell, but with his mouth only, never moving either hand, and seemed to eat it with a satisfaction worthy of his assumed nature. When the oatcake was gone, she set the bowl before him, and he drank the milk with care and neatness, never putting a hand to steady it.

"Now ye must have a sleep, Steenie," said his sister.

She rose, and he crawled slowly after her up the hill on his hands and knees. All the time he kept his face down and his head hanging toward the earth so that his long hair quite hid it. He strongly suggested the look of a great Skye terrier.

When they reached the hut, Kirsty went in and Steenie crept after her. They had covered the floor with heather, the stalks set upright and close packed, so that even where the bells were worn off, it still made a thick, long-piled carpet, elastic and warm. When the door was shut, they were snug there even in winter.

Inside, the hut was about six feet long and four wide. Its furniture was a little pine table and one low chair. In the turf of the wall, Kirsty had cut out a small oblong recess to serve as a shelf for her books. The hut was indeed her library, for in that recess stood almost every book she could call her own. They were about a dozen, several with but one cover, and some with no title, one or two very old, and all well used. Most of her time there, when she was not knitting, Kirsty spent in reading and thinking about what she read. She had read two of Sir Walter's novels and several other things the schoolmaster had lent her. But on her shelf were a Shakespeare, a Milton, and a translation of Klopstock's *Messiah*—which she liked better than the *Paradise Lost*. Among her treasures was also a curious old book of ghost stories, concerning which the sole remark she was ever heard to make was that she would like to know whether they were true. She thought Steenie could tell, but she would not question him about them. Ramsey's *Gentle Shepherd* was there too, which she liked for the good sense in it. There was a thumbed edition of Burns also, but I do not think much of the thumbing was Kirsty's, though she knew several of his best poems by heart.

Between the ages of ten and fifteen, Kirsty had gone to the parish school of the nearest town. It more resembled a village, but they always called it the town. A sister of her father's lived there, and Kirsty was always welcome to spend the night with her, so that she was able to go in most weather. But when she stayed there, her evening was usually spent at the schoolmaster's. Mr. Craig was an elderly man who had married late and lost his wife early. She had left him one child, a delicate, dainty, golden-haired thing, some three or four years younger than Kirsty, who loved her with a protective maternal instinct. Kirsty was one of the born mothers, who are not only of the salt, but are the sugar and shelter of the world. I doubt if little Phemy would have learned anything but for Kirsty. Her father spoiled her a good deal, and never set himself to instruct her, apparently leaving it to the vague tendency of things to make of her a woman like her mother.

He was an excellent teacher. When first he came to Tiltowie, he was a divinity student, but too original ever to become a minister. Such men as would be servants of the church before they are slaves of the church's Master will never be troubled with Mr. Craig's difficulties. For one thing, his strong poetic nature made it impossible for him to believe in a dull, prosaic God. When told that God's thoughts are not as our thoughts, he found himself unable to imagine them inferior to ours. The natural result was that he remained a schoolmaster—to the advantage of many a pupil, and very greatly to the advantage of Kirsty, whose nature was peculiarly open to his influences. The dominie said he had never had a pupil that gave him such satisfaction as Kirsty; she seemed to anticipate and catch at everything he wanted to make hers. There was no knowledge Colin Craig could offer her that the lassie from Corbyknowe would not take inside her like porridge.

In a word, Kirsty learned everything Mr. Craig brought within her reach. When she had once begun to follow a thing, she would never leave the trail of it. Her chief business as well as delight was to look after Steenie, but perfect attention to him left her large opportunity to pursue her studies, especially at such times in which his peculiar affection, whatever it really was, required hours of untimely sleep. For, although at other times he wandered at his will without her, he always wanted to be near her when he slept. During the summer, and as long before and after as the temperature permitted, the hut was the place he preferred, and it was Kirsty's delight to sit in it on a warm day, the door open and her brother asleep on her feet, reading and reading until the sun went down in the sky, filling the hut as it set with a glory of promise, after which came the long gloamin', like a life out of which the light but not the love has vanished. Then indeed she neither worked nor read, but brooded over many things.

Leaving the door open behind them, Kirsty took a book from the shelf and seated herself on the low chair. Instantly Steenie, who had waited motionless until she was settled, threw himself across her feet on the carpet of heather, and in a moment was fast asleep.

There they remained, the one reading, the other sleeping, while the hours of the warm summer afternoon slipped away, like ripples on the ocean of the lovely, changeless eternity, the consciousness of God. After a long time she drew her bare feet from under Steenie and put them on his back, where the coolness was delightful. Then first she became aware that the sun was down and the gloamin' come, and that the whole world must be feeling just like her feet. The long, clear twilight, which would last till morning, was about her, and the eerie sleeping day, when the lovely ghosts come out of their graves in the long grass and walk about in the cool world with little ghostly sighs at the sight of the old places, and fancy they are dreaming.

It was a wonder she could sit so long and not feel worn out. But Kirsty was exceptionally strong, in absolute health, and especially gifted with patience. Because she had so early taken to heart the idea that she was sent into the world to take care of Steenie, devotion to him had grown into a happy habit with her. The waking mind gave itself up to the sleeping, the orderly to the troubled brain, the true heart to the heart as true.

5 / Steenie the Man

There was no difference between the father and mother with regard to this devotion of Kirsty's to Steenie. The mother was especially content with it, for while Kirsty was the apple of her eye, Steenie was her one loved anxiety.

David Barclay was born, like his father and grandfather and many more of his ancestors, on the same farm he now occupied. While his father was still alive, with an elder son to succeed him, David enlisted in the army—mainly from a strong desire to be near a school friend, who was an ensign in the service of the East India Company. Throughout their following military career, they were in the same regiment, the one rising to be colonel, the other to sergeant major. All the time the friendship went on deepening in the men; and all the time was never a man more respectfully obedient to orders than David Barclay to those of the superior officer with whom in private he was on terms of intimacy. As often as they could without attracting notice, the comrades threw off all distinction of rank, and were once again the Archie Gordon and Davie Barclay of old school days.

When they returned to Scotland, both somewhat disabled, the one retired to his inherited estate, the other to the family farm upon that estate, where his brother had died shortly before; so that Archie was now Davie's landlord. But no new relation would ever destroy the friendship that school had made and war had welded. Almost every week the friends met and spent the evening together—much oftener at Corbyknowe than at Castle Weelset. For both married after their return, and their wives were of different natures. And truly the wife at the farm had in her material enough, both moral and intellectual, for ten ladies better than the wife at the castle.

David's wife brought him a son the first year of their marriage, and next came a son to the colonel and a daughter to the sergeant. One night, as the two fathers sat together at the farm, some twelve hours after the birth of David's girl, they mutually promised that the survivor would do his best for the child of the other. Before he died the colonel would gladly have taken his boy from his wife and given him to his old comrade.

As to Steenie, the elder of David's children, he was yet unborn when his father met with a rather serious accident through a young horse in the harvest field, and a false report reached his wife that he was killed. To the shock she thus received was generally attributed the peculiarity of the child, prematurely born within a month after. He had long passed the age at which children usually begin to walk before he would even attempt to stand, but he had grown capable of a speed on all fours that was astonishing. When at last he did walk, it was for more than two years with the air of one who had learned a trick; and throughout his childhood and a great part of his boyhood, he was always more ready to go down on all fours than use his feet.

The sleeping youth began at length to stir, but it was more than an hour before he quite woke up. Then all at once he started to his feet, with his eyes wide open, throwing back from his forehead the long hair that fell over them, and revealing a face not actually looking old, but strongly suggesting age. His eyes were of a pale blue, with a hazy, fixed, uncertain gleam in them, reminding one of the shifty shudder and shake and start of the northern lights. His features were peculiarly small. Although he had been all day acting like a dog in charge of sheep, both his countenance and its expression had a remarkable absence of the animal in his face. He had a kind of exaltation in his look; he seemed to expect something, not at hand but sure to come. His eyes rested for a moment, with a love of absolute devotion, on the face of his sister. Then he knelt at her feet and bowed his head before her. She laid her hand upon it, and in a tender tone said, "Man Steenie!" Instantly he rose to his feet. Kirsty rose also, and they went out of the hut.

The sunlight had not left the west, but had crept round some distance toward the north. Stars were shining through the thin shadows of the world. Steenie stretched himself up, threw his arms aloft, and held them raised, as if all at once he would grow and reach toward the infinite. Then he looked down on Kirsty, for he was taller than she, and, with the long, lean forefinger of one of the long, lean arms that had all day been a leg to the would-be dog, pointed straight up into the heavens and smiled. Kirsty looked up, nodded her head, and smiled in return. Then they started in the direction of home, and for some time walked in silence. At length Steenie spoke. His voice was rather feeble, but clear, articulate, and musical.

"My feet's terrible heavy tonight, Kirsty," he said. "Gien it wasna for them, the rest o' me would be up and away. It's terrible to be holden doon by the feet this way."

"We're a' holden doon the same way, Steenie. Maybe it's worse for ye, as would sae fain go up, than for the rest o' us that's more willin' to bide a wee. But it'll be the same at last when we're a' up there togither."

"I wouldna care sae muckle gien he didna grip me by the ankles like."

"When the right times comes," returned Kirsty, "the bonny man'll loose yer ankles himsel'."

"Ay, ay! I ken that weel. He told me himsel'. I'm thinkin' I'll see him tonight, for I'm sore holden doon and needin' a sight o' him. He's sometimes a lang time comin'!"

Kirsty said no more. Her heart was too full.

Steenie stood still, and throwing back his head, stared for some moments up into the great heavens over him. Then he said, "It's a bonny day, the day the bonny man lives in! The other day—the day the rest o' ye bides in—the day when I'm no mysel' but a sore, uncomfortable collie—that day's too hot—and some-times too cold. But the day he bides in is aye jist what a day should be! Ay, it's that! It's that!"

He threw himself down and lay for a minute looking up into the sky. Kirsty stood and regarded him with loving eyes.

"I hae a' the bonny day afore me!" he murmured to himself. "Eh, but it's better to be a man than a beast. Snootie's a fine beast, and a grand collie, but I would rather be mysel'—a heap rather—aye at hand to catch a sight o' the bonny man! Ye must go hame to yer bed, Kirsty!"

"Willna ye go wi' me, Steenie, as far as the door?" rejoined Kirsty.

It was at such times as this that Kirsty knew sadness. When she had to leave her brother on the hillside all the long night—to look on no human face, hear no human word, but wander in strangest worlds of his own throughout the slow dark hours—the sense of separation would wrap her as in a shroud. In his bodily presence, however far away in thought or sleep or dreams his soul might be, she could yet tend him with her love. But when he was out of her sight, and she had to sleep and forget him, where was Steenie then and how was he faring? At such times he seemed to her as one forsaken, left alone with his sorrows to a companion-less and dreary existence.

But in truth, Steenie was by no means to be pitied. However much his life may have been apart from the lives of other men, he did not therefore live alone. Was he not still of more value than many sparrows? And Kirsty's love for him had in it no shadow of despair. Her pain at such times was but the indescrib-able lovelack of mothers when their sons are far away, and they do not know what they are doing or what they are thinking. And yet how few, when the air of this world is clearest, ever come into essential contact with those they love best! But the triumph of Love, while most it seems to delay, is yet ceaselessly rushing hitherward on the wings of the morning.

"Willna ye go as far as the door wi' me, Steenie?" she said.

"I will. But ye're no feart, are ye?"

"Na, no a grain. What would I be feart for?"

"Ow, naethin'. At this time there's naethin' oot and aboot to be feart at. In what ye call the daytime, I'm a kind o' in danger o' knockin' mysel' against things; I never do that at night."

As he spoke he sprang to his feet, and they walked on. Kirsty's heart seemed to swell with pain; for Steenie was at once more rational and more strange than usual, and she felt the further away from him. His words were very quiet, but his eyes looked full of stars.

"I canna tell what it is aboot the sun that makes a dog o' me," he said. "He's hard-like, and holds me oot, and makes me hang my head, and feel as if I were kind o' ashamed, though I ken naethin'. But the bonny night comes straight up to me and into me, and goes all through me, and bides in me; and then I look for the bonny man!"

"I wish ye would let me bide oot the night wi' ye, Steenie."

"Why, Kirsty. Ye must sleep, and I'm better alone."

"That's jist it!" returned Kirsty with a deep-drawn sigh. "I canna stand yer bein' alone, and yet, do what I like, I canna, even in the daytime, get a bit closer to ye. If only ye was as little as ye used to be, when I could carry ye aboot all day, and take ye into my own bed all night! But noo we're jist like the sun and the moon—when ye're oot, I'm in; and when ye're in—weel, I'm no oot, but my soul's jist as blear-faced as the moon in the daylight to think ye'll be away again sae soon!—But it canna go on like this to all eternity, and that's a comfort!"

"I ken naethin' aboot eternity. I'm thinkin' it'll all turn into a starry night, wi' the bonny man in it. I'm sure o' one thing—that something'll be puttin' right that's far frae right noo. And then, Kirsty, ye'll hae yer own way wi' me, and I'll be sae far like other folk: idiot that I am, I would be sorry to be turned altogither the same as some! Ye see, I ken sae muckle they ken naethin' aboot or they wouldna be as they are."

"We'll all hae to come over to ye, Steenie, and learn frae ye what ye ken. We'll hae to make *you* the minister, Steenie. But some night ye'll let me bide oot wi' ye, willna ye, Steenie?"

"Ye shall, Kirsty. But it must be some night ye hae slept all day."

They went on all the rest of the way talking thus, and Kirsty's heart grew lighter, for she seemed to get a little nearer to her brother. He had been her live doll and idol ever since his mother laid him in her arms when she was little more than three years old. For though Steenie was nearly a year older than Kirsty, she was at that time so much bigger that she was able, not indeed to carry him, but to have him on her knees. She thought herself the elder of the two until she was about ten, by which time she could not remember any beginning to her carrying of him. About the same time, however, he began to grow much faster, and she found before long that only upon her back could she carry him any distance.

The discovery that he was the elder somehow gave a fresh impulse to her love and devotion, and intensified her pitiful tenderness. Kirsty's was indeed a heart in which the whole unhappy world might have sought and found shelter.

6 / Corbyknowe

"Ye'll come in and say a word to Mother, Steenie?" said Kirsty, as they came near the door of the house.

It was a long, low building, with a narrow paving in front from end to end, of stones cast up by the plough. Its walls were but one story high, in rough, cast plaster and whitewashed, and they shown dim in the twilight. Under a thick projecting thatch, the door stood wide open, and from the kitchen, whose door was also open, came the light of a peat fire and a fish-oil lamp. Throughout the summer Steenie was seldom in the house an hour out of the twenty-four, and now he hesitated to enter. In the winter he would keep about it a good part of the day, and was generally indoors the greater part of the night, but by no means always.

While he hesitated, his mother appeared in the doorway of the kitchen. She was a tall, fine-looking woman, with soft gray eyes, and an expression of form and features that left Kirsty accounted for.

"Come away in, Steenie, my man," she said, in a tone that seemed to wrap its object in fold upon fold of tenderness, enough to make the peat smoke that pervaded the kitchen the very atmosphere of the heavenly countries. "Come and hae a drappy o' the new-milked milk, and a piece o' breid."

Steenie stood smiling and undecided on the slab in front of the doorstep.

"I would rather no come in tonight, and no trouble ye more wi' the sight o' me—that is, till the change come and things be set right. I dinna aye ken what I'm aboot, but I aye ken that I'm

42

a kind o' a disgrace to ye, though I canna tell hoo I'm to blame for it. Sae I'll jist bide ootside wi' the bonny stars that ken all aboot it, and doesna think the worse o' me."

"Laddie! laddie! who on the face o' God's earth thinks the worse o' ye for a wrong done ye?—though who has the fault o' that I darena think, weel kennin' that all things either ordered or allowed, makin' muckle the same thing. Come winter, come summer, come right, come wrong, come life, come death, what are ye, what can ye be but my own laddie!"

Steenie stepped across the threshold and followed his mother into the kitchen, where the pot was on the fire for the evening's porridge. To hide her emotion she went straight to it and lifted the lid to see whether the boiling point had arrived. The same instant the stalwart form of her husband appeared in the doorway, and there stood for a moment.

He was a good deal older than his wife, as his long gray hair, among other witnesses, testified. He was six feet in height, and very erect, with a rather stiff military carriage. His face wore an expression of stern goodwill, as if he had been sent to do his best for everybody, and knew it.

Steenie caught sight of him before he had taken a step into the kitchen. He rushed to him, threw his arms round him, and hid his face against his chest.

"Bonny, bonny man!" he murmured, then turned away and went back to the fire.

His mother was casting the first handful of meal into the pot. Steenie fetched a three-legged stool and sat down by her, looking as if he had sat there every night since first he was able to sit.

The farmer came forward and drew a chair to the fire beside his son. Steenie laid his head on his father's knee. Not a word was uttered. The mother might have found them in her way had she been inclined, but the thought did not occur to her, and she went on making the porridge in great contentment, while Kirsty set the table. The night was as still in the house as in the world, except for the bursting of the big blobs of the porridge. The peat fire made no noise.

At length the mother took the heavy pot from the fire, and, with what to one who had not seen her do it a hundred times might have seemed wonderful skill, poured the porridge into a huge wooden bowl on the table. Having then scraped the pot carefully so that nothing should be lost, she poured some water into it and set it on the fire again, went to a hole in the wall, took out two eggs, and placed them gently in it.

Next she went to the dairy and came back with a jug of the richest milk, which she set beside the porridge. Then they all drew their seats to the table—all but Steenie.

"Come, Steenie," said his mother, "here's yer supper."

"I dinna care aboot any supper tonight, Mother," answered Steenie.

"Godsake, laddie, I kenna hoo ye live!" she returned in a tone almost of despair.

"I'm thinkin' I dinna need sae muckle as ither fowk," rejoined Steenie, whose white face bore testimony that he took far from enough nourishment. "Ye see I'm no a' there," he added with a smile, "sae I canna need sae muckle."

"There's enough o' ye there to fill me heart plenty full," answered his mother with a deep sigh. "Come, Steenie, my bairn!" she went on coaxingly. "Yer father winna eat a mouthful if ye dinna: ye'll see that! Eh, Steenie," she broke out, "if ye would but take yer supper and go to bed like the rest o' us! It makes my heart break to think o' ye oot in the mirk night! Who's to tell what mightna be happenin' to ye!"

"I'll bide in, if that be yer will," replied Steenie; "but eh, if ye kenned the difference to me, ye wouldna wish it. I seldom sleep at night as ye ken, and in the hoose it's jist as if the darkness got inside o' me and was chokin' me!"

"But it's as dark ootside as in the hoose—sometimes anyway."

"Na, Mother. It's never sae dark oot but there's light enough to ken I'm there and no in the hoose. I can aye draw a good full breath oot in the open."

"Let the laddie go his own way, wuman," interposed David. "The thing born in him's better for him than the thing born in another. A man must go as God made him."

"Ay, whether he be man or dog!" assented Steenie solemnly.

He drew his stool close to his father where he sat at the table, and again laid his head on his knee. The mother sighed but said nothing. She did not look hurt, only very sad. In a minute Steenie spoke again.

"I'm thinkin' none o' ye kens," he said, "what it's like when all the hillside's full o' the ither ones."

"What ither ones?" asked his mother. "There can be none there but yer own lonely sel'."

"Ay, there's the rest o' us," he rejoined, with a wan smile.

The mother looked at him with something almost of fear in her eyes of love.

"Steenie has company we ken little aboot," said Kirsty. "I sometimes think I would give him my wits for his company."

"Ay, the bonny man," murmured Steenie. "—I must be gaein'!"

But he did not rise, did not even lift his head from his father's knee: it would be rude to go before the supper was over—especially since he was not partaking of it.

David had eaten his porridge, and now came the almost nightly difference about the eggs. Marion had been watching the perfect time to take them from the pot, but when she would as usual have her husband eat them, he as usual declared he neither needed nor wanted them. This night, however, he did not insist, but at once proceeded to prepare one, which, as soon as it was nicely fixed with salt, he began to feed to Steenie. The boy had been longer used to being thus fed than most children, and now took the first mouthful instinctively, and then moved his head, but without raising it from his knee, so that his father could feed him more comfortably. In this position he took every spoonful given him, and so ate both eggs, greatly to the satisfaction of all the rest of the company.

A moment more and Steenie got up. His father rose also.

"I'll go wi' ye a bit, my man," he said.

"Eh, na! Ye needna do that, Father. It's nearhand yer bedtime. I'll jist be aboot in the night—maybe a stane's throw frae the door, maybe the other side o' the Horn. Here or there I'm never far frae ye. I sometimes think I'm jist like one o' them that ye call dead: I'm no away, I'm only dead."

So saying, he went. He never wished them good night: that would be to leave them, and he was not leaving them! He was with them all the time.

7 / David and His Daughter

The instant Steenie was gone, Kirsty went a step or two nearer to her father.

"I saw Francie Gordon today, Father."

"Weel, lassie, I reckon that wasna any strange occurrence. Whaur did ye see him?"

"He came to me on the Hornside, whaur I sat knittin' my stockin', over the bog on his pony—a right bonny thing and clever—a new one he's gotten from his mither. And it's no the first time he's been there to see me since he came home."

"What for did he visit ye there? My door's always open to him."

"He wanted to see me alone."

"He wanted you, did he? And he's been more than once after ye? Why didna ye tell me afore, Kirsty?"

"We were bairns together, ye ken, Father, and I never once thought the thing worth botherin' ye aboot till today. We've aye been used to Francie comin' and gaein'! But today he spoke straight oot, and I laughed at him, and angert him, and then he angert me."

"And why are ye tellin' me noo?"

" 'Cause I thought maybe it would be best—no that it makes any difference I can see."

During their conversation Marion was washing the supper things, putting them away, and making general preparations for bed. She heard every word and went about her work softly that she might hear, never opening her mouth to speak.

"There's something ye want to tell me that ye dinna like, lassie," said David. "Ye're no feart o' speakin' to yer father?"

"Feart at my father! I might be gien I had anything to be ashamed o'. When I'm feart at you, Father, I'll be a good way on toward the ill way," returned Kirsty, looking straight into her father's eyes.

"Then it'll never be, or I must hae a heap to blame mysel' for. I sometimes think, gien bairns kenned the terrible blame their fathers might hae to suffer for noo doin' better wi' thee, they would be more particular to hold straight. I hae been too muckle taken up wi' my beasts and my crops—more, God forgive me, than wi' my two bairns. Though, God kens, ye're more to me than anything else save the mother o' ye!"

"The beasts and the crops couldna weel do wi' less if there was aye oor mither to see after us, but who else was to see to puttin' food on the table?"

"That's true, lassie. I only hope it wasna greed in my heart! At the same time, who would I be greedy for but yersel's?— Weel, what's it all aboot? What made ye come to me aboot Francie? I must admit, I'm some feart at him noo that he's so much oot o' oor sight. The laddie's no by nature an ill laddie—far frae it. But it's a sore pity he couldna hae been all his father's and none o' his mither's."

"That wouldna hae been sae weel contrived," remarked Kirsty.

"But what's this aboot Francie?"

"Ow naethin', Father, worth mentionin'. The daft loon would hae had me promise to marry him—that's a'!"

"The Lord preserve us! Jist off hand, wi'oot preparation?"

"There's no tellin' what might hae been in his head. He didna get sae far as to say that."

"God forbid!" exclaimed her father.

"I'm thinkin' God's forbid it long since," rejoined Kirsty.

"What did ye say to him, lassie?"

"First I laughed and called him the gowk he was. And then I

sent him away wi' an earful o' what I had to say; for he had the
impudence to fall oot on me for carin' more aboot Steenie than
the likes o' him. As if he could come within sight o' Steenie!"

Her father looked very grave.

"Are ye no pleased, Father? I did what I thought right."

"Ye couldna hae done better, Kirsty. But I'm sorry for the
lad, for I loved his father. For his father's sake I could take Francie
into the hoose, and work for him as for ye and Steenie—though
it's little good Steenie gets o' me, poor soul."

"Dinna say that, Father. It would be an ill thing for Steenie
to hae onybody but yersel' to be the father o' him. He makes it
through a muckle part o' the night frae the love o' ye and his
mither."

"And yersel', Kirsty."

"I hae my share in the daytime, nae doobt."

"And hoo, do ye think, goes the rest o' the night wi' him?"

"The bonny man has the most o' it, I dinna doobt, and what
better would we wish for him! But, Father, gien Francie comes
back again wi' the same thing, what would ye hae me say to
him?"

"Say what ye will, lassie, sae long as ye dinna let him for the
moment believe there's a grain o' possibility in the thing. Ye see,
Kirsty—"

"Ye dinna imagine, Father, I could for a moment think otherwise aboot it than ye do yersel'. Don't I ken that his father gave
ye charge o' him, and haena I therefore to look after him as weel?
I'm very sure his father would never approve o' any gaeins on
between him and a lassie such like mysel'."

"Gladly would I show Francie the road to such a wife as you
would make him, my bonny Kirsty. But ye see clearly the thing's
no to be thought upon, but no on accoont o' yer no bein' good
enough for him. For that ye are, good enough for any man! But
it's grand to an auld father's heart to hear ye take yer part in his
promise in such a wumanly fashion!"

"Am I noo yer own lass-bairn, Father? Whaur would I be wi'

a father that didna keep his word? And what less could I do than help any man to keep his word? Would ye hae me tell the laddie's mither? I wouldna like to expose the folly o' him, but gien ye think it necessary, I'll go.''

"I dinna think that would be weel. It would but raise a strife between the two, wi'oot doing an atom o' good. She would only rage at the laddie, and so anger him that they would almost never come togither again. And though ye went and told her yersel', the lady would lay blame on you nonetheless. There's no reason in the poor body.''

"I'm glad ye dinna want me to go," said Kirsty. "She carries hersel' so grand that ye're almost driven to consider her worth the less; and that's no the right spirit to have toward anyone God thought worth makin'.''

8 / Castle Weelset

By the time he reached home, Francis' anger had died down a good deal. As his father's friend had said, he was by no means a bad sort of fellow; only he was full of himself, and therefore of little use to anybody. He and his mother were constantly on the edge of a quarrel. Both of them must have their own way or argue. Francis' way was sometimes good, his mother's sometimes not bad, but both were usually selfish.

The boy had fits of generosity; the woman never did, except toward her son. If she thought of something to please him, well and good! If he wanted anything of her, it would never do! The idea must originate with her. If she imagined her son desired a thing, she felt it something she could never grant, and told him so. But thereafter Francis would never rest until he had got it. Sudden division and high words would follow, with silence toward the boy on the mother's part waiting in the wings, which might upon occasion last for days. Becoming all at once tired of it, she would one morning appear at breakfast looking as if nothing had ever come between them, and they would be the best of friends for a few days, or perhaps a week, seldom longer. Then some new discord, usually not much different in character from the preceding, would arise between them, and the same weary round be tramped all over again, each always in the right, and the other in the wrong. It hardly seemed possible things should be able to go on thus indefinitely.

In matters of looks, which Francis had the tendency to care about too greatly, his mother's own vanity led her to indulge and spoil him, for, being hers, she was always pleased when he looked his best. On his real self she neither had nor sought any influence. Arrogance in him, as long as it was not directed toward her own dignity, actually pleased her. She liked him to show his spirit: was it not a mark of his breeding?

She was a tall and rather stout woman, with a pretty, small-featured, regular face, and a thin nose with the nostrils pinched.

Castle Weelset was not much of a castle. A rather large, defensible house had been added in the last century to an ancient round tower, uncomfortably habitable on its own. It stood on the edge of a gorge, crowning one of its stony hills of no great height. With hardly a tree to shelter it, the situation was very cold in winter, and it required a hardy breeding to live there in anything resembling comfort. There was a little garden, and the stables were somewhat ruinous. For the smallness of the former the climate almost sufficiently accounted, and for the latter a long period of comparative poverty.

The young laird did not like farming, and had no love for books. In this interval between school and college, he found very little to occupy him, and not much to amuse him. Had Kirsty been as encouraging as he had expected, he would have made use of his new pony for nothing more than to ride to Corbyknowe in the morning and back to the castle at night.

His mother knew old Barclay, as she called him, well enough—that is, not at all, and had never shown him the least cordiality, indeed nothing better than condescension. She would not even treat him as a gentleman when he sat at her own table. He had never been to the castle since the day after her husband's funeral, when she treated him with such emphasized superiority that he felt he could not go again without running the risk either of having his influence with the boy ruined, or giving occasion to a nature within himself that he was trying his best to put to death.

From that time on, therefore, he was content with giving Francis a pleasant welcome to his farm, and doing what he could to make his visits enjoyable. Chiefly on such occasions the boy delighted in drawing from his father's friend what tales about his father, and adventures of their campaigns together, he had to tell. In this way David's wife and children heard many things about himself that would not otherwise have reached them. Naturally Kirsty and Francis grew to be good friends, and after they went to the parish school, there were few days indeed on which they did not walk as far homeward together as the midway divergence of their roads would permit. It is not, therefore, altogether strange that the time would come at length when Francis should fancy himself in love with Kirsty.

But I believe all the time, he thought of marrying her as a heroic deed, in raising the girl his mother despised to share the lofty position he and his foolish mother imagined him to occupy. The anticipated opposition of his mother naturally strengthened his determination. He had not dreamed of opposition on the part of Kirsty. He took it as a mere matter of course that the moment he stated his intention, Kirsty would be charmed, her mother more than pleased, and the stern old soldier overwhelmed with the honor of alliance with the son of David's colonel. I do not doubt, however, that in addition to this, he did have an affection for Kirsty far deeper than either of them realized. Although it was mainly his pride that suffered in his humiliating dismissal, I am sure he had a little genuine heartache as he galloped home as well. When he reached the castle, he left his pony to go where it would, and rushed to his room. He locked the door so that his mother would not enter, and threw himself on his bed in the luxurious consciousness of a much-wronged lover. An uneducated country girl, for so he regarded her, had cast from her, not without insult, his splendidly generous offer of himself!

Poor King Cophetua did not, however, shed many tears for the loss of his beggar-maid. By and by he forgot everything, found he had gone to sleep, tried to weep again, but did not succeed.

He soon grew hungry and went down to see what was to be had. It was long past the usual hour for dinner, but Mrs. Gordon had not seen him return.

"Gracious, you've been crying!" she exclaimed the moment she saw him.

Now certainly Francis had not cried much. But his eyes were a little red.

He had not yet learned to lie, but he might then have made his first attempt had he had a fib at his tongue's end. As he had not, he grew yet gloomier, and made no answer.

"You've been fighting!" said his mother.

"I haena!" he returned with rude indignation. "Gien I had been, do ye think I would hae cried?"

"You forget yourself, laird!" said Mrs. Gordon, more annoyed with his use of Scotch than the tone of his voice. "I would have you remember I am mistress of this house!"

"Till I marry, Mother!" rejoined her son.

"Oblige me in the meantime," she rejoined, "by leaving such vulgar language outside the walls of it."

Francis was silent, and his mother, content with her victory, and in her own untruthfulness of nature believing that he had indeed been fighting and had the worst of it, said no more, but began to pity and pet him. A pot of his favorite jam with a dish of crisp sweetened oatcakes presently consoled the love-wounded hero.

9 / David and Francis

One day there was a market at a town some eight or nine miles away, and for lack of anything else to do, Francis went there to display himself. He was riding his pony with so tight a curb that the poor thing every now and then reared in protest against the agony he suffered.

On one of these occasions the pony Don was about to fall backward, when a brown wrinkled hand laid hold of him by the head, half-pulling the reins from his rider's hands; and before the young man had quite settled himself again, the man belonging to the aged hand had unhooked the chain of the horse's curb and fastened it some three links looser. Francis was more than indignant, even when he saw that the hand was Mr. Barclay's.

"Hoots, my man!" said David gently, "there's no occasion to put a water chain on the bonny beastie. He has a mouth like a leddy's, and to hae it linked up sae tight is naethin' less than torture to him. It's a wonder to me he hasna broken yer bones and his own back togither, poor thing!" He patted and stroked the spirited little creature that stood sweating and trembling.

"I thank you, Mr. Barclay," said Francis angrily. "But I am quite able to manage the brute myself. You seem to take me for a fool."

"Indeed, he's no far off bein' one that could call a bonny creature like that a brute," returned David, hardly pleased to discover such hardness in one whom he would gladly treat like a child of his own. It was a great disappointment to him to see the lad getting further away from the possibility of being helped by him. "What would yer father say to see ye ill use any helpless bein'! Yer father was awful good to his horsefowk."

The last word was one of David's own making: he was a great lover of animals.

"I'll do with my own as I please!" cried Francis, and spurred the pony to pass David. But one stalwart hand held the pony fast, while the other seized his rider by the ankle. The old man was now thoroughly angry with the graceless youth.

"God bless my soul!" he cried. "Hae ye spurs on as weel? Stick one o' them into him again and I'll throw ye frae the saddle. In the thick o' a fight, the long blades playing aboot yer father's head like lights in the north, he never stuck a spur into his charger needlessly!"

"I don't see," said Francis, who had begun to cool a little, "how he could have enjoyed the fight much if he never forgot himself."

"Yer father, laddie, never forgot anything but himsel'. Forgettin' himsel' left him free to mind everything else. *Ye* would forget everything but yer own rage. Yer father was a great man, as weel as a great soldier, Francie, and a de'il to fight, as his men said. I hae mysel' seen by his set mouth and clenched teeth that he was boilin' inside, when all the time on the brow o' him sat never a wrinkle. Gien ever there was a man that could think o' two things at once, yer father could think o' three; and those three were God, his enemy, and the beast beneath him. Francie, Francie, in the name o' yer father, I beg ye to regard the rights o' the neighbor ye sit upon. Gien ye dinna, afore long ye'll come to think little o' yer human neighbor as weel, carin' only for what ye get oot o' him."

A voice inside Francis took part with the old man, and made him yet angrier. Also his pride was the worse annoyed that David Barclay, his tenant, should, in the hearing of two or three loafers gathered behind him, of whose presence the old man seemed totally unaware, not only rebuke him, but address him by his first name, and the diminutive form of it besides. So when David, in the appeal that burst from his enthusiastic remembrance of his officer in the battlefield, let the pony's head go, Francis dug his spurs in its sides and darted off like an arrow. The old man for a moment stared after him with an open mouth. The fools around laughed. He turned and walked away, his head sunk in disappointment.

Francis had not ridden far before he was vexed with himself. He was not so much sorry as he was annoyed that he had behaved in such an undignified fashion. The thought that his childish behavior would justify Kirsty in her opinion of him added to its sting. He tried to console himself with the reflection that the sort of thing ought to be put an end to at once; otherwise, how far might not the old fellow's interference go! I am afraid he even said to himself that such was the consequence of familiarity with inferiors. Yet angry as he was, he would have been proud of any approval from the lips of the old soldier. He rode his pony mercilessly for a mile or so, then pulled up and began to talk gently to it, which I doubt if the little creature found consoling, given the state of its mouth.

About halfway home, he had to ford a small stream or else go around two miles by a bridge. There had been a great deal of rain in the night, and the stream was considerably swollen. As he approached the ford, he met a knife grinder who warned him not to attempt it: he had nearly lost his wheel in it, he said. But Francis always found it hard to accept advice, as did his mother. So when she often predicted evils, which never followed, he had come to think counsel the one thing not to be heeded.

"Thank you," he said; "I think we can manage it!" and rode on.

When he reached the ford, where of all places the pony's head ought to have been free, he foolishly thought of the curb chain again, dismounted, and took it back up a couple of links.

But when he remounted, whether from dread of the rush of the brown water or resentment at the threat of renewed torture, the pony would not take the ford. A battle royal arose between them, in which Francis was so far victorious that, after many attempts to run away, little Don, rendered desperate by the spurs, dashed wildly into the stream. He went plunging along for two or three yards and fell, and suddenly Francis found himself rolling in the water, swept along by the current.

A little way lower down, at a sharp turn of the stream under a high bank, was a deep pool. It was a place dreaded by the country children, fearing it was a haunt of the kelpie. Francis knew the spot well and had good reason to fear it, for he could not swim. He struggled yet harder at the thought of it, succeeded in recovering a portion at least of his footing, and managed to get out on the shore, but lay on the bank for a while, exhausted. At length he came to himself and rose, found nothing of his pony to be seen, and still the water was between him and home. If the youth's good sense had been equal to his courage, he might have been a fine fellow. He dashed straight into the ford, floundered through it, and lost his footing no more than little Don would have had he been treated properly. When he reached the high ground on the other side, he could still see nothing of the pony, and with sad heart concluded it carried into the Kelpie's Hole, never more to be seen. What would his mother and Mr. Barclay say! Shivering and miserable, and with a growing guilt in his conscience over his treatment of Don, Francis dragged himself wearily home.

Don, however, had never been much in danger. Rid of his master, he could take good enough care of himself. He got to the bank without difficulty, and took care it should be on the home side of the stream. He did not once look behind him for his tyrant, but set off at a good trot, much refreshed by his bath, and made for his loose-box at Castle Weelset.

In a narrow part of the road, however, he overtook a cart of Mr. Barclay's. Attempting to pass between it and the high bank, the pony's bridle was caught by the driver's hand, making the horse a prisoner. Tying him to the cart behind, the man then took him to Corbyknowe. When David came home and saw him, he conjectured pretty nearly what happened, and, tired as Mr. Barclay was, set out for the castle. Had he not feared that Francis might have been injured, he would not have cared to go, as much as he knew it would relieve the boy to know his pony was safe.

Mrs. Gordon declined to see David, but he learned from the servants that Francis had come home half-drowned, leaving Don in the Kelpie's Hole.

David hesitated a little, wondering whether or not to punish him for his behavior to the pony by allowing him to remain in ignorance of its safety. But he finally concluded that such was not his part, and told them that the animal was safe at Corbyknowe, and went home again. He wanted Francis to fetch the pony himself, therefore did not send it, and in the meantime fed and groomed it with his own hands as if he had been his friend's charger. Francis had just enough of the grace of shame to make him shrink from going to Corbyknowe in person, and asked his mother to write to David, asking him why he did not send home the animal, and she gladly did. David, one of the most courteous of men, would take no order from any but his superior officer, and answered that he would gladly give the pony up to the young laird in person.

The next day Mrs. Gordon drove, in what state she could muster, to Corbyknowe. Once there, she declined to leave her carriage, requesting Mrs. Barclay, who came to the door, to send her husband out. Mrs. Barclay thought it best to comply.

David came a few minutes later in his shirt-sleeves.

"If I understand your answer to my request, Mr. Barclay, you decline to send back Mr. Gordon's pony. Pray, on what grounds?"

"I wrote, ma'am, that I should be glad to give him over to Mr. Francis himself."

"Mr. Gordon does not find it convenient to come all this way on foot. In fact, he declines to do it, and requests that you will send the pony home this afternoon."

"Excuse me, mem, but it's surely enough done that a man make known the presence o' strays, and take proper care o' them till they're claimed. I was jist tryin' to give the bonny thing a bit o' pleasure in life. Francie's too hard on him."

"You forget, David Barclay, that Mr. Gordon is your landlord!"

"His father was my landlord, and his father's was my father's landlord. And the interests o' the landlord hae aye been oors. Other than Francie's hearty friend I could never be!"

"You presume on my late husband's kindness to you, Barclay!"

"Gien devotion be presumption, mem, I presume. Archibald Gordon was and is my friend, and will be forever. We hae been through too muckle togither to change one anither. It was for his sake and the laddie's own that I wanted him to come to me. I wanted a word wi' him aboot that pony o' his. He'll never be a true man that takes no notice o' the dumb animals."

"I will have no one interfere with my son. I am quite capable of teaching him his duty myself."

"His father requested me to do what I could for him, mem."

"His *late* father, if you please, Barclay!"

"He'll never be Francie's *late* father gien I can help it, mem. He may be yer *late* husband, mem, but he's still my colonel, and I'll keep my word to him. It willna be long, in the nature o' things, till I go to him, and would well like to answer him: 'Archie, I ken naethin' aboot the laddie but what I could hae wished o' him!' Hoo would ye like to give sich an answer yersel', mem?"

"I'm surprised at a man of your sense, Barclay, thinking we shall know one another in heaven! We shall have to be content with God there!"

"I said naethin' aboot heaven, mem. Fowk may ken one anither and no be in the same place. I took note in the kirk last Sunday that Abraham kenned the rich man, and they werena togither in one place. But ye'll let the yoong laird come and see me, mem?" concluded David, changing his tone and speaking as one who begged a favor; for the thought of meeting his old friend and having nothing to tell him against his son quenched his pride.

"Home, Thomas!" cried her late husband's wife to her coachman, and drove away.

"They'll hae to give that wife a hell to hersel'!" said David, turning to the door discomfited.

"She'll no like it when she has it!" returned his wife, who had heard every word. "There's fowk that's no fit company for onybody, and I'm thinkin' she's sich a one if there be no other."

"I'll send Jemie home wi' the pony tonight," said David. "A body canna insist whaur fowk are no friends. That would grow to enmity, and put an end to any good. Na, we must send home the pony, and if there be any grace in the bairn, he canna but come and say thank ye."

Mrs. Gordon rejoiced in what she supposed her success, but David's yielding showed itself the true victory. Francis did call and thank him for the care of Don. He even granted that perhaps he had been too hard on the pony.

"Ye could hardly expect naethin' o' a pony o' his size that pony o' yers couldna do, Francie," said David. "But in God's name, dear laddie, be a righteous man. Gien ye require no more than's fair frae man or beast, ye'll mostly aye get it. But gien yer ootlook in life be to get all things and give naethin, ye must come to grief one way and all ways. Success in an ill attempt is the worst failure a man can make."

But it was talking to the wind, for Francis thought David was, like his mother, only bent on finding fault with him. He made haste to get away, and left his friend with a sad heart.

He rode on to the foot of the Horn, to the spot where Kirsty was usually to be found at that season. But she saw him coming and went farther up the hill.

Soon afterward, his mother contrived that he should pay a visit to some relatives in the south, and for a time neither the castle nor the Horn saw anything of him. Without returning home, in the winter he went to college in Edinburgh, where he neither disgraced nor distinguished himself. David was glad to hear no ill of him. To be beyond his mother's immediate influence was perhaps to his advantage, but as nothing superior was substituted, it was at best little gain. His companions were like himself, such as might turn to worse or better, no one could tell which.

10 / Kirsty and Phemy

During the first winter Francis spent at college, his mother was south in England, and remained there all the next summer and winter. When at last she came home, she was even less pleasant than before in the eyes of her household, no one of which had ever loved her. Throughout the summer she had a succession of visitors, and stories began to spread concerning strange doings at the castle. The neighbors talked of extravagance, and some of them of riotous living. A few of the servants more than hinted that the amount of wine and whiskey consumed was far in excess of that served when the old colonel was alive.

One of these servants who acted as housekeeper in her mistress's frequent fits of laziness had known David Barclay from his boyhood, and understood his real intimacy with her late master. It was therefore hardly surprising that she should open her mind to him, though toward everyone else she kept a settled silence concerning her mistress's affairs: none of the stories circulating about the countryside came from her. But David was to Mrs. Bremner the other side of a deep pit, into the bottom of which whatever was said between them dropped forever.

"There'll come a catastrophe afore long," said Mrs. Bremner one evening when David had overtaken her on the road to the town. "The property's jist away to the dogs! There's Master Donal, the factor, gaein' aboot like one no kennin' whether to cut his throat or blow his brains oot. He dares not say a word, ye see. The auld laird trusted him, and he's feart at being blamed, but there's na doin' anything wi' that wuman: he's got to give her the siller when she wants it!"

"The siller's no hers any more than the land; all's the yoong laird's," remarked David.

"That's true, but she has the power o' it till he comes o' age. And Master Donal, poor man, many's the time he's jist driven to his limit wi' what's wanted o' him. And what comes o' the siller I canna think: there's no a thing aboot the hoose to show for it. And hearken, David, but dinna let both yer ears hear it—I'm no doobtin' that the drink's gettin' a grip o' her."

"I wouldna be none surprised," returned David. "Whatever might want in at her door, there's naethin' inside to hold it oot. Eh, to think o' Archie Gordon takin' to himsel' sich a wife! That a man like him, o' good reputation, and come to years o' discretion—to think o' brains like his turnin' as spongy as an auld turnip at sight o' a bonny front to a hoose wi' but one well! It canna be that witchcraft's clean done away wi'!"

"Bonny, David! Did ye call the mistress bonny?"

"She used to be—bonny, that is, as a button or a buckle might be bonny. What she may be noo, I dinna ken, for I haena set eyes upon her since she came to the Knowe orderin' me to send back Francie's pony. She was supercilious enough for two colonels and a corporal, but no ill lookin'. Gien she hae a spot o' beauty left, the drink'll take it before it hae done wi' her."

"It's taken the color frae her already, an' begun to give her anither! But it concerns me more aboot Francie than my leddy. What's to come o' him when all's gone? What'll there be for him to come into?"

Gladly would David have interfered, but he was helpless. He had no legal guardianship over or for the boy. Nothing could be done till he was a man—"if ever he be a man!" said David to himself with a sigh, and the thought came to him of how much better off he was with his half-witted Steenie than his friend with his clever Francie.

Mrs. Bremner was the schoolmaster's sister-in-law, and was at that moment on her way to see him and her little niece, Phemy. From childhood the girl had been in the habit of going to the castle to see her aunt, and so was well known about the place. Being an engaging child, she had become not only welcome to the servants, but something of a favorite with the mistress, whom she amused with her little airs and pleased with her winning manners. She was now about fourteen, a half-blown beauty of the red and white, gold and blue kind. She had long been a vain little thing, approving of her own looks in the mirror, and taking much interest in them, but so simple as to make no attempt to conceal her self-satisfaction. Her pleased expression while admiring herself, and the frantic attempts she made to get sight of her back when wearing a new dress, were indeed more amusing than hopeful, but her vanity was not yet so pronounced as to overshadow her better qualities. Kirsty had thought it best not to point it out; although, being more than anyone else a mother to her, she was already a little anxious about it, especially in that neither her aunt nor her father saw nor imagined the least fault in her.

The fact that the child had no mother drew the heart of Kirsty, whose own mother was her strength and joy. At the same time, Kirsty's gratitude to the child's father, who had opened for her some doors of wisdom and knowledge, moved her to make what return she could for the eternal obligation she felt. It deepened her sense of debt to Phemy that the schoolmaster did not do for his daughter anything like what he had for years been doing for his pupil. From this Kirsty almost felt as if she had diverted to her own use much that rightly belonged to Phemy. Yet she knew very well that even had she never existed, the relationship between the father and the daughter would have been the same. The child of his dearly loved wife, the schoolmaster was utterly content with his Phemy. He felt as if she knew everything her mother knew, had the same inward laws of being, and the same disposition, and was simply, like her, perfect.

It was an inconceivable idea to him that she should ever do anything wrong. Nor was there much chance of his discovering it if she did. When not at work, he was constantly reading. Most people close a book without having gained from it a single germ of thought; Mr. Craig, however, seldom opened one without falling directly into some mental study over something suggested by it. But I believe that, even when thus absorbed, Phemy was never far from his thought. At the same time, like many Scots, he seldom showed her much affection, seldom made an effort to show her how much he loved her. He took for granted that his love was understood by her.

Since he had all his life not been able to live without learning because of the instinctive love of knowledge within him, it had never even occurred to the man that his child might need to be taught. For she did not quite share his passion.

Kirsty tried to make up for his neglect, but could not do nearly what she would have liked. The child did not take to learning. And though she loved Kirsty and wanted to please her, she could not be made to stick to her tasks in Kirsty's absence. Kirsty had her to the farm as often as the schoolmaster would permit, and Phemy was always glad to go to Corbyknowe. Had Kirsty been backed by the child's father, she might have made something of her, but she worried about Phemy's future when she would be able to have less and less influence with her.

Phemy was rather afraid of Steenie. Her sunny nature shrank from the shadow, as of a wall, in which Steenie appeared to her always to stand. She would involuntarily recoil from any little attention he would offer her, though she was never rude to him, and he soon learned to leave her undismayed. Kirsty could see plainly that the child's repugnance troubled him, though he never spoke of it; she could read his face like a book. Kirsty's eyes were constantly looking at him, feeding like sheep on the pasture of his face. But I should say rather—the thoughts that strayed over his face were the sheep to which all her life she had been the devoted shepherdess.

At Corbyknowe things went on as before. Kirsty was in no danger of tiring of the even flow of her life. Steenie's unselfish solitude of soul made him every day dearer to her. She sought books wherever she thought she might find them. She had no thought of distinguishing herself, and not even the smallest ambition of becoming learned. Her soul was thirsty to understand, and what she understood found its way from her mind into her life. Her keen power and constant practice of observation greatly benefited her thinking.

Personally I utterly refuse the notion that we cannot think without words, but certainly the more forms we have ready to embody our thoughts, the further we shall be able to carry our thinking. Richly endowed, Kirsty required the more mental food, and was the more able to use it when she found it. To such of the neighbors as had no knowledge of any diligence except that of the hands, she seemed to lead an idle life. But indeed, even Kirsty's hands were far from idle. When not with Steenie she was almost always at her mother's call, who, from the fear that she might grow up incapable of managing a house, often required a good deal of her. She would quickly lay her book aside and eagerly jump up whenever she was summoned. But once dismissed, she would at once take up her book again. She could read anywhere, and gave herself none of the student airs that make some young people so pitifully unpleasant from trying to show how much they know. At the same time solitude was preferable for study, and Kirsty was always glad to find herself with her books in the little hut, Steenie asleep on the heather carpet on her feet, and the assurance that there no one would interrupt her.

It was not so strange, then, that in the sweet absence of selfish cares, and her mind full of worthy thoughts and her heart going out in all directions in tenderness, her face should go on growing in beauty and refinement. She had not yet arrived at full physical growth, and the forms of her person being therefore in a process of change were the more easily modeled after her spiritual nature. She seemed almost already to be one of the kind that would not die but would live forever, continuing to inherit the earth throughout all eternity. Neither her father nor her mother could have imagined anything better to be made of her.

Steenie had not changed his habits, neither seemed to grow at all more like other people. He was now less frequently unhappy and seldom so much depressed. But he showed no sign of less dependence on Kirsty.

11 / The Earth House

About a year after Francis Gordon went to Edinburgh, Kirsty and Steenie made a discovery.

Between Corbyknowe and the Horn, on whose sides David Barclay had a right of pasturage for the few sheep to which Steenie and Snootie were the shepherds, was a small valley, or glen. Through it ran a little brook on its way to join the little lake above with the little river below, and along the banks of this stream lay two narrow breadths of nice grass. The brother and sister always crossed this brook when they wanted to go straight to the top of the hill.

One morning, having each taken the necessary run and jump across the brook, they had begun to climb up on the other side, when Kirsty heard an exclamation from Steenie, who was a few paces behind her.

"It's the weight o' my muckle feet!" he cried, as he dragged one of the troublesome members out of a hole in the soft turf. "Losh. I dinna ken hoo far it mightna hae gone if I hadna gotten a hold o' it in time and pulled it oot!"

How much of humor, how much of silliness, and how much of the truth were wrapped up together in some of the things he said, it was impossible to determine.

"If ye set yer foot in a hole," said Kirsty, "what can it do but go doon in it?"

"But there was nae hole!" returned Steenie. "My foot jist went doon and made it. Look there! I went in almost to my knee!"

"Let's look," said Kirsty, and proceeded to examine the place.

At first she thought it must be the burrow of some animal. She began to pull away the heather about the mouth of the opening. Steenie set himself to help her. Kirsty was by far the stronger of the two, but Steenie always did his best to help her in anything that required exertion.

They soon saw the lump of sod and heather that Steenie's heavy foot had driven down; and when they pulled it out, they saw that the hole went deeper still, seeming to be a very large burrow indeed—almost a little fearsome. They widened the mouth of it by clearing away a thick growth of roots from its sides, took out a quantity of soft earth, and realized that it went sloping into the ground still farther. With growing curiosity they leaned down into it lying on the edge, and reaching with their hands, removed the loose earth as low as they could. This done, the descent showed itself about two feet square, as far down as they had cleared it, beyond which after a little way it was lost in the dark.

What were they to do now? Their curiosity impelled them to go on, and immediately! But there were other considerations. Kirsty knew that Steenie had a horror of dark places, associating them somehow with the weight of his feet. Whether such places had for him any suggestion of the grave, I cannot tell. Certainly to get rid of his feet was the form his idea of the salvation he needed was readiest to take. And what if there was some animal inside? Steenie doubted it, for there was no opening until he made it; and Kirsty doubted it also, on the ground that she knew no wild animal larger than fox or badger, neither of which would have made such a big hole. But her imagination almost succeeded in getting the best of her: what if some huge bear had been asleep in it for hundreds of years, and growing all the time? Certainly he could not get out, but if she roused him, and he got hold of her! The next instant her courage revived, however. The passage must lead somewhere, she reasoned, and it was large enough for her to explore it!

Because of her dress, she had to creep in head first—in which lay the advantage that if there was any danger, she would meet it face to face. She told Steenie that if he heard her cry out, he must get hold of her feet and pull. Then she lay down on the ground and crawled in. She thought it must lead to an ancient tomb, but said nothing of her idea for fear of horrifying Steenie, who stood trembling by.

She went down into the earth, and disappeared. Not a foot was left for Steenie to lay hold of. The time seemed long and terrible to him as he stood there forsaken, his Kirsty out of sight in the heart of the earth. He knew there had been wolves in Scotland once: who could tell but a she-wolf had been left, and a whole clan of them lived there underground, never coming out in the daytime? There might be another opening somewhere else on the hill, under a rock, and hidden by heather!

At length the faithful fellow forgot his fear and was half inside the hole to go after her when up shot the head of Kirsty almost in his face. For a moment he was terribly perplexed. He had been expecting to come on her feet, not her head: how could she have gone in head first and not come back feet first?

"Eh!" he said, "it's awful to see ye come oot o' the earth like a muckle worm!"

"Ye saw me go in, Steenie, ye gowk!" returned Kirsty.

"Ay, but I didna see ye come oot! Eh, Kirsty, hae ye a head at both ends o' ye?"

Kirsty's laughter blew Steenie's discomposure away, and he too laughed.

"Come back home," said Kirsty. "I must get a candle. Yon's a place that must be seen into. I never saw, or rather felt the like o' it."

"What is there room for?" asked Steenie.

"For you and me, and twenty or thirty more, maybe—I dinna ken," replied Kirsty.

"I want none o' it," returned Steenie.

"I'll go doon wi' the candle," said Kirsty, "and see whether it be a place for ye. If I cry oot, 'Ay, it is,' will ye come?"

"Ay, that I will, if it were the whale's belly!" replied Steenie.

They set off for the house, and as they walked they talked.

"I wonder what the place could ever hae been for!" said Kirsty, more to herself than Steenie. "It's bigger than I could imagine."

"What's it like, Kirsty?" inquired Steenie.

"Hoo can I tell when I saw naethin'," replied Kirsty. "But," she added thoughtfully, "if it werena that we're in Scotland and they're in Rome, I would hae been most sure I had got into one o' the catacombs."

"Oh, losh!" 'cried Steenie, "I canna bide the very word o' the creatures!"

"What word?" asked Kirsty, a little surprised, for how did Steenie know anything about the catacombs?

"To think," he went on, "o' a whole kirk o' cats beneath the earth—all sittin' combin' themselves wi' combs! Kirsty, ye *winna* think it a place for *me*? Ye see, I'm not like other fowk, and such a thing might drive me oot o' the small wits I ever had!"

"Hoots!" rejoined Kirsty with a smile, "the catacombs hae naethin' to do wi' cats or combs!"

"What are they then?"

"The catacombs was what in auld times, and not in this century even, they called the places where they laid their dead."

"Oh, Kirsty, but that's even worse!" returned Steenie. "I wouldna go into such a place wi' feet like mine—no, not for all the world could give me! I would never get my feet oot o' it. They'd hold me there!"

Then Kirsty began to tell him, as she would have taught a child, something of the history of the catacombs, knowing how it would interest him.

"In the days long ago," she said, "there was fowk, like you and me, unco fond o' the bonny man. The very sound o' the name o' him was enough to make their hearts leap wi' doonright gladness. And they went here and there and told everybody aboot him, and fowk that didna ken him, and dinna want to ken him, couldna bide to hear tell o' him, and they said, 'Let's hae nae more o' this! Hae done wi' yer bonny man. Hold yer tongues,' they cried. But the others, they wouldna hear o' holdin' their tongues. Everybody must ken aboot him! 'Sae long as we hae tongues, and can use them to tell aboot him,' they said, 'we'll not hold them.' And at that they fell upon them and ill-used them dreadful. Some o' them they took and burnt alive—that is, burnt them dead. And some o' them they flung to the wild beasts, and they bit them and tore them to bits. And—''

"Did the bitin' o' the beasts hurt terrible?" interrupted Steenie.

"Ay, I reckon it did. But the poor fowk aye said that the bonny man was wi' them, and let them bite—they didna care!"

"Ay, o' coorse, if he was wi' them, they wouldna mind a hair, or at least not two hairs! Who would! If he be in yon hole, Kirsty, I'll go back and into it myself. I will noo!"

Steenie turned and had run some distance before Kirsty succeeded in stopping him. She did not run after him.

"Steenie! Steenie!" she cried. "I dinna doobt he's there, for he's everywhere. But ye ken yersel' ye canna aye see him; and maybe ye wouldna see him there noo either, and might think he wasna there, and turn back afraid. Wait till we hae a light, and I'll go doon first."

Steenie was persuaded, and turned and came back to her. He was always obedient to father, mother, and sister.

"Ye see, Steenie," she continued, "yon's no the place. I dinna ken yet what yon place is. I was only going to tell ye aboot the places it reminded me o'. Would ye like to hear aboot them?"

"Right well, I would! Say away, Kirsty!"

"Weel, ye see, the fowk that loved the bonny man got themselves aye togither to have talk wi' one another aboot him. And as I was tellin' ye, the fowk that didna care aboot him were that angert that they set upon them. So to keep oot o' their grip, they counseled togither, and concluded to gather in a place where naebody would think o' lookin' for them—where but in the bowels o' the earth, where they laid their dead upon shelves in the rock.''

"Oh, but that was fearsome!" interposed Steenie. "They must hae been sore determined! If I had been there, would they hae made me go wi' them?"

"No, not if ye didna like. But ye would hae liked weel to go, for they built up the shelves, ye ken. It was hollowed oot— whether oot o' hard earth or soft stone, I dinna ken, I reckon it would be some no so hard kind o' a rock—and when the dead was laid in it, they built up the mouth o' the place, that is, frae that same shelf to the one that was above it, and so it was weel closed in.''

"But what for didna they bury their dead sensible-like in their kirkyards?"

" 'Cause theirs was a great muckle toon, wi' such a heap o' houses that there wasna room for kirkyards. So they took them ootside the toon, and went underground wi' them altogither. For there they hollowed oot a lot o' passages, and here and there a wee room-like, wi' their halls going frae them this way and that. So when they took themselves there, the friends o' the bonny man would fill one o' the little roomies, and stand in all the passages that went frae it. And that way, though there couldna many o' them see one another at once, a gey lot o' them would hear. For there they could speak oot loud, and a body above would hear naethin' and suspect naethin'. And jist think, Steenie, there's a picture o' the bonny man himsel' painted on the wall o' one o' those places doon beneath the ground.''

"I reckon it'll be unco like him!"

"I canna tell aboot that.''

"If I could see it, I could tell. But I'm thinkin' it'll be some far away.''

"Ay, it's far. It would take a body—let me see—maybe half a year to travel there on his own feet," answered Kirsty, after some thought.

"And me longer, my feet's so heavy," remarked Steenie with a sigh.

As they drew near the house, their mother saw them coming and went to the door to meet them.

"We're wantin' a bit o' candle, Mother," said Kirsty.

"Ye can hae that," answered Marion. "But what do ye want a candle for in the broad middle o' the daylight?"

"We want to go doon a hole," replied Steenie with flashing eyes, "and see the picture o' the bonny man."

"Hoot, Steenie! I told ye it wasna there," interposed Kirsty.

"Na," returned Steenie, "ye only said yon hole wasna that place. Ye said the bonny man *was* there, though I mightna see him. Ye didna say the picture wasna there."

"The picture's not there, Steenie. We've come upon a hole, Mother, that we want to go doon into and see what it's like," said Kirsty.

"The weight o' my feet broke through into it," added Steenie.

"Preserve us, lassie! Be careful whaur ye carry the bairn!" cried the mother. "But, eh, weel I ken ye'll take him nae place but whaur it's weel he should go. The laddie needs two mithers, and the Merciful has given him two. Ye're as much his mither as me, Kirsty."

She asked no more questions, but got them the candle and let them go. They hastened back, Steenie in his most jubilant mood, which seemed always to have in it a touch of deathly frost and a flash as of the primal fire. What could be the strange displacement or maladjustment which, in the brain harboring the immortal thing, troubled it so and made it yearn after an untasted liberty? The source of his jubilance now was easy to tell: the idea of the bonny man was henceforth, in that troubled brain of his, associated with the place into which they were about to descend.

The moment they reached the spot, Kirsty, to the renewed astonishment of Steenie, dived at once into the ground at her feet and disappeared.

"Kirsty! Kirsty!" he cried out after her, and danced about like a terrified child. Then he shook with a fresh dismay at the muffled sound that came back to him in answer from the unseen hollows of the earth.

Already Kirsty stood at the bottom of the sloping tunnel and was lighting her candle. When it lit up, she found herself looking into a level gallery, the roof of which she could touch. It was not an excavation, but had been trenched from the surface, for it was roofed with great slabs of stone. Its sides, of rough stones, were six or seven feet apart at the floor, which was paved with small boulders, but sloped so much toward each other that at the top their distance was less by about two and a half feet. Kirsty was, as I have said, a keen observer, and her power of seeing had been greatly developed through her constant conscientious endeavor to realize every description she read.

She went on about ten or twelve yards, and came to a bend in the gallery, succeeded by a sort of chamber, from which branched a second gallery, which soon came to an end. The place was in truth not unlike the catacombs; only its two galleries were built and much wider than the excavated thousands in the catacombs. She turned back to the entrance, there left her candle lit, and again startled Steenie, still staring into the mouth of the hole, with her sudden appearance.

"Would ye like to come doon, Steenie?" she said. "It's a queer place."

"Is it awful fearsome?" asked Steenie, shrinking back.

His feeling of dismay at the cavernous, sub-earthly dark was not inconsistent with his pleasure in being out on the wild waste hillside when heaven and earth were absolutely black, not seldom the whole of the night, in utter loneliness to eye or ear, without ever feeling anything like dread. Then and there only did he seem to have room enough. His terror was of the smallest pressure on his soul, the least hint at imprisonment. That he could not rise and wander about among the stars at his will shaped itself to him as the heaviness of his feet holding him down. His feet were the loaded chains that made of the world but a roomy prison. The limitless was essential to his conscious well-being.

"Not a bit," answered Kirsty, who felt awe anywhere—on a hilltop, in a churchyard, in sunlit room—but never fear. "It's as like the place I was telling ye aboot—"

"Ay, the cat place!" interrupted Steenie.

"The place wi' the picture," returned Kirsty.

Steenie darted forward, shot head first into the hole as he had seen Kirsty do, and crept undismayed to the bottom of the slope. Kirsty followed close behind, but he was already on his feet when she joined him. He grasped her arm eagerly, his face turned from her, and his eyes gazing fixedly into the depth of the gallery, lighted so vaguely by the candle on the floor of its entrance.

"I think I saw him!" he said in a whisper full of awe and delight. "I think I did see him!—but, Kirsty, hoo am I to be sure that I saw him?"

"Maybe ye did and maybe ye didna see him," replied Kirsty. "But that doesna matter sae muckle, for he's aye seein' you, and ye'll see him, and be sure that ye see him, when the right time comes."

"Ye do think that, Kirsty?"

"Ay I do," returned Kirsty confidently.

"I'll wait then," answered Steenie, and in silence followed Kirsty along the passageway.

This was Steenie's first, and all but his last descent into the *earth house*, or *Picts' house*, or *weem*, as a place of the sort is called. There are many such in the east of Scotland, their age and origin objects of merest conjecture.

The moment Steenie was out of it, he fled to the Horn.

The next Sunday he heard read at church the story of the burial and resurrection of the Lord, and, unavoidably after their talk about the catacombs, associated the chamber they had just discovered with the tomb in which "they laid him." At the same time he concluded that the top of the hill, where he had, as he believed, on certain favored nights met the bonny man, was the place from which he ascended, to come again as he did! From that moment on the earth house no longer had any attraction for Steenie. The bonny man was not there; he was risen! He was somewhere above the mountaintop haunted by Steenie, and

Steenie already knew that the man sometimes descended upon it, for had not Steenie seen him there?

Happy Steenie! Happier than so many Christians who, more in their brain senses but far less in their heart senses than he, haunt the sepulchre as if the dead Jesus still lay there, and forget to walk the world with him who dieth no more, the living one!

But his sister took a great liking to the place, and was not repelled by the mistaken suspicion that there the people of the land, in past times unknown, had buried some of their dead. In the hot days, when the earth house was cool, and in the winter when the thick blanket of snow lay over it, and it felt warm as she entered it from the frosty wind, she would sit there in the dark, sometimes imagining herself one of the believers of the old time thinking the Lord was at hand, coming in person to fetch her and her friends. When the spring came, she carried down sod and turf, and made for herself a seat in the central room, there to sit and think. By and by she fastened an oil lamp to the wall, and would light its rush-pith wick and read by it. Occasionally she made a good peat fire, for she had found a chimney that went sloping into the upper air, and if it did not always draw well, peat smoke is as pleasant as it is wholesome, and she could bear a good deal of its smoldering and smokiness. Often she took her books there when no one was likely to want her, and enjoyed to the full the rare and delightful sense of absolute safety from interruption. Sometimes she would make a little song there, with which as she made it, its own tune and music would come; and she would model the air with her voice as she wrote the words in a little book on her knee.

12 / A Visit From Francis Gordon _____

The summer following Gordon's first session at college, Castle Weelset and Corbyknowe saw nothing of him. No one missed him much, and but for his father's sake no one would have thought much about him. Kirsty, as one who had told him the truth about himself, thought of him oftener than anyone except her father.

The next summer he paid a short visit to his home, and went one day to Corbyknowe. He left a favorable impression on everyone, and Kirsty had been all the more favorably disposed to him because of the respect she felt for him as a student. His old overbearing tendency that made him so unlike his father had retired into the background. His smile, though not so sweet, came oftener, and his carriage was full of courtesy. But something was gone, which his old friends missed. His behavior in the old times was not so pleasant, but he had been as one of the family. Often disagreeable, he was yet loving. Now, however, he laid himself out to make himself acceptable as a superior. Finally away from his mother's lowering influence, what was of his father in him might by this time have come more to the surface but for certain ladies in Edinburgh—connections of the family, who were influenced by his good looks and pleasant manners, and possibly by his position in the Gordon country—sought his favor by deeds of flattery, and succeeded in spoiling him.

Steenie happened to be about the house when he came, and Francis behaved so kindly to him that the gentle creature, overcome with grateful delight, begged him to go to see a house he and Kirsty were building.

In some families the games of the children mainly consist in the construction of dwellings of this kind or that—castle or ship or cave or wood-fort or nest in a treetop—according to the material attainable. It is an outcome of the aboriginal necessity for shelter, this instinct of burrowing. Northern children cherish in their imaginations the sense of protection more, I fancy, than others. This is partly owing to the severity of their climate: the snow and wind, the rain and sleet, the hail and darkness they encounter. I doubt whether an English child can ever have the sense of protection as a Scot's bairn in bed on a winter night, his mother in the nursery, and the wind howling like a pack of wolves about the house.

Francis consented to go with Steenie to see his house, and Kirsty naturally accompanied them. By this time she had gathered the little that was known, and there is very little known yet, concerning *Picts' houses*; and as they went it occurred to her that it might be pleasant to the laird to be shown something on his own property of which he had never heard, and which, in the eyes of many, would add to its value. Therefore she took the way that led past the earth house.

She had so well cleared out its entrance that it was now comparatively easy to get into; otherwise I doubt if the young laird would have risked the spoiling of his admirably fitting clothes to satisfy the mild curiosity he felt regarding Kirsty's discovery. As it was, he pulled off his coat before entering, despite her assurance that he "needna fear blaudin' anything."

She went in ahead of him to light her candle and he followed. As she showed him the curious place, she gave him the results of her reading about such constructions. Then she told him how Steenie had led the way to its discovery. By the time she ended, Gordon was really interested—chiefly, no doubt, in finding himself possessor of a thing that many learned men would think worth coming to see.

"Did you find this in it?" he asked, seating himself on her little throne of turf.

"Na, I put it there mysel'," answered Kirsty. "There was naethin' in the place, jist naethin' at all. Ye couldna hae telled whatever it was meant for—hoose or byre or barn or kirk or kirkyard. It hae been jist a hiding hole in troubled times when the country would be swarmin' wi' marauders, that's what I'm thinkin'."

"Why did ye make the seat, Kirsty?" asked Gordon, falling into the mother tongue with a flash of his old manner.

"I come here sometimes," she answered, "to be alone and read a bit. It's sae quiet. Eternity seems itsel' to come and hide in it sometimes. I'm sometimes tempted to bide the night."

"Isna it awful cold?"

"Na, no that often. It's fine and warm in the winter. And I can light a fire when I like. But ye haena yer coat on, Francie. I oughtna to hae let ye bide so long."

He shivered, rose, and made his way out. Steenie stood in the sunlight waiting for them.

"Ay, Steenie," said Gordon, "you brought me to see your house. Why didn't you come in with me?"

"Na, na! I'm feart for my feet: this is no *my* hoose!" answered Steenie. "I'm buildin' one. Kirsty's helpin' me. That's what ye had to see, no this one. This is Kirsty's hoose. It was Kirsty wanted ye to see this one."

Steenie turned and flew up the hill.

"Where does he want to take me, Kirsty? Is it far?" he asked.

"Ay, it's a gey bit. It's nearly at the top o' the Horn, a wee beyond it."

"Then I shall not go," returned Francis. "I will come another day."

"Steenie! Steenie!" cried Kirsty. "He'll not go today. He says he'll come anither time. But I'll join ye by and by at yer hoose."

Steenie went on up the hill, and Kirsty and Francis walked toward Corbyknowe.

"Has no young man appeared yet to cut Steenie's nose out of joint about you, Kirsty?" asked Gordon.

Kirsty thought the question rude, but answered with quiet dignity. "No one. I never had muckle opinion o' *young men*, and dinna care aboot their company. But what are ye thinkin' o' doin' yersel!'—I mean, when ye're through wi' the college?" she continued. "Ye'll surely be comin' home to take things into yer ain hand? My father says sometimes he's afraid they're no bein' made the most o'."

"The property must look after itself, Kirsty. I will be a soldier like my father. If it could do without him when he was in India, it may just as well do without me. As long as my mother lives, she shall do what she likes with it."

Thus talking, and growing more friendly as they went, they walked slowly back to the house. There Francis mounted his horse and rode away, and for more than two more years they saw nothing of him.

13 / Steenie's House

Steenie seemed always to experience a strange sort of terror while waiting for anyone to come out of the earth house, into which he never entered, and it was his fear of the place that chiefly moved him to build a house of his own. He may also have calculated on being able, with such a refuge at hand, to be on the hill in any kind of weather. They still made use of their little hut as before, and Kirsty still kept her library in it, but it was at the foot of the Horn, and Steenie loved the peak of it more than any other spot in his narrow world. For himself, he would like a house on the very top of the Horn, not one inside it like Kirsty's.

Near it was a little scoop out of the hillside, sheltered on all sides except the south. Here, it is true, were no flowers to weave a pattern upon its carpet of green. True also here were no beautiful angels, in green wings and green garments, poised in the sweet night air, watchful with their short, pointless, flaming swords against the creeping enemy. But it was nevertheless the loveliest carpet of grass and moss.

On the northern slope of the hollow, full in the face of the sun, a little family of rocks had fallen together, odd in shapes and positions, but of long stable equilibrium, with narrow spaces between them. The sun was throwing its last red rays one day among these rocks when Steenie wandered into the little valley. The moment his eyes fell upon them, he said in his heart, "Yon's the place for a hoose. I'll get Kirsty to build one, and maybe she'll come and stay in it wi' me sometime!"

In his mind there were for some years two conflicting ideas

of refuge: one embodied in the heathery hut with Kirsty, the other typified by the uplifted loneliness, the air and the space of the mountain upon which the bonny man sometimes descended. For the last three years or more the latter idea had the upper hand. Now it seemed possible to have the two kinds of refuge together, where the more material would render the more spiritual easier to attain! Such were not Steenie's words; indeed, he used none concerning the matter. But such were his vague thoughts— feelings rather, not yet thoughts.

The spot had indeed many advantages. For one thing, the group of rocks was the ready skeleton of the house Steenie wanted. Again, if the snow sometimes lay deeper there than in other parts of the hill, there first it began to melt. A third advantage was that, while, as I have said, the valley was protected by higher ground everywhere but on the south, it there afforded a large view over the boggy basin and over the hills beyond its immediate rim, to a horizon in which stood some of the loftier peaks of the highland mountains.

When Steenie's soul was able for a season to banish the nameless forms that haunt the dim borders of insanity, he would sit in that valley for hours, regarding the wider-spread valley below him, in which he knew every height and hollow. And, with his exceptionally keen sight, he could see signs of life where another would have beheld nothing but dead space. Not a live thing, it seemed almost, could spread wing or wag tail, but Steenie would become thereby aware of its presence. Boasting to her parents of Steenie's faculty, Kirsty said to her father one day, "I dinna believe, Father, wi' Steenie on the bog, a red worm could stick up his head oot o' it wi'oot him seein' it!"

Steenie set about his house-building at once, and when he had got as far as he could without her, called for help from Kirsty, who never interfered with and never failed him. Divots he was able to cut out of the peat, and he provided a good quantity of them, but when he came to moving stones, two pairs of hands were often needed. Indeed, before the heavier work of "Steenie's hoosie" was over, the two had to beg the help of more—of their father and of men from the farm.

During its progress, Phemy Craig paid a long visit to Corbyknowe and often joined the two in their labor on the Horn. She was not very strong, but would carry a good deal in the course of a day, and through this association with Steenie, her dread of him gradually vanished, and they became friends.

When Steenie's design was at length carried out, they had built up with stone and lime the open spaces between several of the rocks. They had cased these walls outside with something like plaster, lined them inside with softer and warmer walls of cuttings from the green sod of the hill, and had covered in the whole as well as possible—very irregularly no doubt, but smoothing all the corners and hollows with turf and heather. This done, one of the men, who was a good thatcher, fastened the whole roof down with strong lines so that the wind could not get under and strip it off. The result was a sort of burrow, consisting of several irregular compartments with open communication. They included one small rock inside. Steenie would make it serve for a table and some of its inequalities for shelves. In one of the recesses they contrived a fireplace, and in another a tolerably well-concealed exit. Steenie, like a trapdoor spider, could not endure the thought of only one way out: one way was enough for getting in, but two were necessary for getting out, his best refuge being the open hill.

The night came at length when Steenie would take formal possession of his house. In his heart was a solemn, silent jubilation. It was soft and warm, in the middle of the month of July. The sun had been set about an hour when he got up to leave the parlor, where the others always sat in the summer, and where Steenie would now and then appear among them. As usual he said good night to no one of them, but stole gently out.

Kirsty knew what was in his mind, but was careful not to show that she took any notice of his departure. As soon as her father and mother retired, however, when he had been gone about half an hour, she put aside her work and hastened out. She felt a little anxious about him, though she could not have said why.

Folded in the twilight, Earth lay as still and peaceful as if she had never done any wrong, or never seen anything wrong in one of her children. There was light everywhere, and darkness everywhere to make it strange. A pale-green gleam prevailed in the heavens, as if the world were a glowworm that sent abroad its home-born radiance into space and colored the sky. In the green light rested a few small solid clouds with sharp edges, and almost an assertion of repose. Throughout the night it would be no darker. The sun seemed already to have begun to rise, only he would be all night about it. From the door she saw the point of the Horn clear against the green sky. Steenie would be up there soon. He was hurrying on his way! Sometimes he went very leisurely, stopping and gazing, or sitting down to think. But he would not do that tonight! But she could walk faster than he, and would not be long behind him.

The sky was full of pale stars, and as she went, Kirsty amused herself by arranging them into shapes and mathematical figures. The only star Steenie knew by name was the pole star, which, however, he always called *The bonny man's lantern*.

She had climbed the hill, and was drawing near the house, when she was startled by a sound of something like singing, and stopped to listen. She had never heard Steenie attempt to sing, and the very thought of his doing so moved her greatly: she was always expecting something marvelous to show itself in him. She drew nearer. It was not singing, but it was something like it, or something trying to be like it—a succession of broken, harsh, imperfect sounds, with here and there a tone of brief sweetness. She thought she perceived in it an attempt at melody, but the many notes that refused to be made prevented her from finding the melody intended, or the melody, rather, after which he was feeling. The broken music ceased suddenly, and a different kind of sound succeeded.

She went yet nearer. He could not be reading. She had tried to teach him to read, but the genuine effort he put forth to learn made his head ache and his eyes feel wild, he said, and she at once gave up the endeavor.

He had been accustomed to hear his father pray—always extempore—and such he was attempting now. Prayer, with Steenie, as well as with Kirsty, was the utterance, audible or silent, in the ever-open ear, of what was moving in him at the time. This was what she now heard him say:

"Bonny man, I ken ye weel: there's naebody in heaven or earth that's like ye. Ye ken yersel' I would jist die for ye if ye wanted it o' me, but I'm hopin' that ye winna want it o' me, I'm that awful coowardly. Oh, take the fear oot o' my heart an' make me ready to do what ye want o' me, weighty feet an' all, wi'oot thinkin' twice aboot it. And, eh, bonny man, willna ye come doon sometime an' walk the hill here so that I may see ye? Eh, if ye was but once to look in at the door o' this hoose o' mine that ye hae given me! If ye were to look in at the door an' cry *Steenie!* soon would ye see whether or no I was in the hoose. I thank ye for this hoose. I'm goin' to hae a rich an' happy time on this hill! Eh, bonny man, gie a look in the face o' my father an' mither in their bed ower at the Knowe, an' I pray ye see that Kirsty's gettin' a fine sleep, for she has a heap o' trouble wi' me. She's so clever—as ye ken, for ye made her! An' look ower this bit hoose that I call mine an' that they helped me to build, even though it's jist a wee lean-to—jist as all the hooses are jist bairn's hooses built by themsel's aboot the big floor o' yer kitchen an' in the nooks o' the same—wi' yer own truffs an' stanes an' divots."

Steenie's voice ceased, and Kirsty, thinking his prayer had come to an end, knocked at the door, so that her sudden appearance would not startle him. From his knees, as she knew by the sound of his rising, Steenie sprang up and came darting to the door with the cry, "It's the bonny man!"

Oh, how sorry was Kirsty to stand where the loved of the human was not. She almost turned and fled.

"It's only me, Steenie," she faltered, nearly crying.

Steenie stood and stared. For a moment neither could speak.

"Eh, Steenie," said Kirsty at length, "I'm right sorry I disappointed ye. I didna ken what I was doin'."

"Ye couldna help it," answered Steenie. "Ye couldna be him, but ye're the next best, and right welcome. I'm as glad as can be to see ye, Kirsty."

Kirsty followed him inside in silence.

"Maybe ye're him after all," said Steenie. "He can take any shape he likes. I wouldna wonder if ye was him! Ye're unco like him anyway!"

"Na, na, Steenie! I'm far frae that! But I would like to be what he would hae me, jist as ye would yersel'."

This was the man's hour, not the dog's, yet Steenie threw himself at her feet.

"Go oot by yersel', Steenie," she said, caressing him with her hand. "That's what ye like best, I ken. Ye needna mind me. I only came to see ye settled in yer own hoose. I'll bide a bit. Go oot, and ken that I'm in the hoose, and that ye can come back to me when ye like."

"Ye're aye right, Kirsty," answered Steenie, rising. "Ye aye ken what I'm needin'. I must get oot, for I'm some chokin' like— but jist come here a minute first," he went on, leading the way to the door. There he pointed up into the wild of stars and said, "Ye see yon star on the top o' that other one that's brighter?"

"I see it fine," answered Kirsty.

"Weel, when that starnie comes right ower the white top o' yon stone in the middle o' that side o' the hollow, I'll be here at the door."

Kirsty looked at the stone, saw that the star would arrive at the point indicated in an hour, and said, "Weel, I'll be expectin' ye, Steenie."

Whereupon he departed, going farther up the hill to court the soothing of the heaven.

In conditions of consciousness known only to himself and incommunicable, the poor fellow sustained an all but continuous hand-to-hand struggle with insanity, more or less agonized according to the nature and force of its varying assault; in which struggle, if not always victorious, he had yet never been defeated. Often tempted to escape misery by death, he had hitherto stood firm. Some part of every solitary night was spent, I imagine, in fighting that other evil suggestion. Doubtless what kept him lord of himself through all the truth-aping delusions that usurped his consciousness was his unyielding faith in the bonny man.

The name by which he so constantly thought and spoke of as the savior of men was not of his own finding. The story was well known of the idiot who, having partaken of the Lord's supper, was heard murmuring to himself as he retired, "Oh, the bonny man! the bonny man!" And there were many persons, sound in mind as large of heart, who thought the idiot might well have seen him who came to deliver them that were bound. Steenie took up the tale with a most believing mind. Never doubting the man had seen the Lord, he responded with the passionate desire himself to see *the bonny man*. It awoke in him while yet quite a boy, and never left him, but increased as he grew, and became a fixed idea, a sober waiting, an unebbing passion, urging him to righteousness and lovingkindness.

Kirsty took from her pocket a book and sat absorbed in it until the star attained its goal, and suddenly there was Steenie by her side. She shut the book and rose.

"I'm a heap better, Kirsty," said Steenie. "The color's away doon the stairs, an' the soft wind made its way oot o' the sky an' come to me. Sae noo I'm jist as weel as there's any need to be this side o' the darkness. It helped me a heap to ken ye was sittin' there: I could aye run to ye if I wanted. Noo, go to yer ain bed an' take a good sleep. I'm thinkin' I'll be home for breakfast."

"Weel, Mother's goin' to the toon in the morn, and I'll be needin' my strength; I may as weel go," answered Kirsty, and without a good night or farewell of any sort, for she knew how he felt about leave-takings, Kirsty left him and went slowly home. The moon was up and so bright that every now and then she would stop for a moment and read a little from her book, then walk on thinking about it.

From that night, even in the stormy dark of winter, Kirsty was not nearly so anxious about Steenie away from the house. On the Horn he had his place of refuge, and she knew he never ventured on the bog after sunset. He always sought her when he wanted to sleep in the daytime, but he was gradually growing quieter in his mind, and Kirsty had reason to think he slept a good deal more at night.

But the better he grew the more he had the look of one expecting something. Kirsty often heard him saying to himself, "It's comin'! It's comin'!"

"And at last," she said, telling his story many years later, "at last it came, and behind it, I doobtna, came the face o' the bonny man!"

14 / Phemy Craig

Things went on in the same way for four years more, the only visible change being that Kirsty seldom went about barefooted.

She was now between twenty-two and twenty-three. Her face, whose ordinary expression had always been quiet, was now in general quieter still. But when heart or soul was moved, it would flash and glow as only such a face could. Live revelation of deeps rarely rippled except by the breath of God: how could it but grow more beautiful! Cloud or shadow of cloud was hardly to be seen upon it.

Her mother, much younger than her father, was still well and strong, and Kirsty, still not much needed at home, continued to spend the greater part of her time with her brother and her books. As to her person, she was now in the first flower of harmonious womanly strength. Nature had indeed done what it could to make her a lady, but nature was not her mother, and Kirsty's essential ladyhood came from higher up, namely from the Source itself of nature. Simple truth was its crown, and grace was the garment of it. To see her walk or run was to look on the divine idea of motion.

As for Steenie, he looked the same loose lank lad as before, with a smile almost too sad to be a smile, and a laugh in which there was little hilarity. His pleasures were no doubt deep and high, but seldom, even to Kirsty, manifested themselves except in the afterglow.

The schoolmaster's daughter, Phemy, was now almost a woman, of between nineteen and twenty years. She was rather little, but had a nice figure, which she knew instinctively how to show to advantage. Her main charm lay in her sweet complexion—strong in its contrast of colors, but wonderfully perfect in the blending of them. The gradations in the live picture were exquisite. She was gentle of temper, with a shallow, birdlike friendliness, an accentuated confidence that everyone meant her well, which was very enchanting.

But she was far too pleased with herself to be a necessity to anyone else. Her father grew more and more proud of her, but remained entirely independent of her. Kirsty could not help wondering at times how he would feel were he given one peep into the chaotic mind that he fancied so lovely a cosmos. A good fairy godmother would for her discipline, I imagine, turn her into the prettiest wax doll, but with real eyes, and put her in a glass case for all to admire, until she sickened of her very consciousness. But despite Phemy's vanity, Kirsty loved the pretty doll, and cherished any influence she had with her against a possible time when it might be sorely needed. Therefore, she still encouraged Phemy to come to Corbyknowe to visit as often as she felt the desire to. Her father never interfered with any of her goings and comings. But Kirsty had recently begun to notice that Phemy did not care so much for being with her as she once had.

Phemy had been, of course, for some time, the focal point of interest to many neighboring eyes, but had taken only the more pleasure in the attention, none in the persons with the eyes, all of whom she regarded as much below her. To herself she was the only young lady in Tiltowie, an assurance strengthened by the fact that no young man had yet ventured to show a serious interest in her, which she took as a general admission of their social inferiority. In consequence, she behaved to all the young men all the more sweetly.

The tendency of a weakly artistic nature to occupy itself much with its own dress was largely developed in her. It was wonderful, considering the smallness of her father's income, how well she arrayed herself. She could make a scanty material go a great way in setting off her attractions. She possessed, however, another faculty on which she prided herself far more, her ignorance and vanity causing her to mistake it for a grand accomplishment—the faculty of verse-making. She inherited a certain portion of her father's rhythmic and rhyming gift. She could string words almost as well as she could string beads, and many thought her clever because she could do what they could not. Her aunt thought her verses marvelous, and her father considered them full of promise. The minister, on the other hand, judged them unmistakably silly— as her father would have had they not been hers. Only the poorest part of his poetic equipment had propagated in her, and had he taught her anything, she would not have overvalued it so much.

She was herself so full of mawkish sentimentality, how could her verses not fail to be foolish, their whole impulse being the ambition that springs from self-admiration. She had already begun to look down on Kirsty—who would so gladly have been a mother to the motherless creature—for the most untrue of reasons: she was not a lady! Neither in speech, manners, nor dress was she or her mother *genteel*. Their free, hearty, simple bearing, in which there was neither the smallest roughness nor the least suggestion of affected refinement, was not to Phemy's taste; and she began to assume condescending ways. Such changes usually begin to occur in those who have no faintest notion of what *true* ladyhood actually is.

It was, of course, a humiliation to Phemy to have an aunt in Mrs. Bremner's humble position. But she loved her after her own feeble fashion. And although she would occasionally have willingly avoided her, she went not infrequently to the castle to see her, for the kind-hearted woman spoiled her. Not only did she adore her beauty, and stand amazed at her wonderful cleverness, but she also drew out of her little store a good part of the money that went to adorn the pretty butterfly. At the same time she gave her the best of advice, and imagined she listened to it. But the young who take advice are almost beyond the need of it. Fools must experience a thing themselves before they will believe it; and then, remaining fools, they wonder that their children will not heed their testimony. Faith is the only charm by which the experience of one becomes a vantage ground for the start of another.

One day Phemy went to Castle Weelset to see her aunt, and walking down the garden to find her, met the young laird.

Through respect for the memory of his father, he had just received from the East India Company a commission in his father's regiment, and having in about six weeks to pass the slight examination required and then sail to join it, he had come to see his mother and bid her goodbye. He was a youth no longer, but a handsome young fellow, with a pale face and a rather weary, therefore what some would call an interesting, look. For many months he had been leading an idle life.

He lifted his hat to Phemy, looked again, and recognized her. They had been friends when she was a child, but since he saw her last she had grown into a young woman. She was gliding past him with a pretty bow, and a prettier blush and smile, when he stopped and held out his hand.

"It's not possible!" he said. "You can't be little Phemy! Yet you must be!—why, you're a grown lady! To think how you used to sit on my knee. How is your father?"

Phemy murmured a shy answer. She was a little goose, but blushed as a very flamingo. In her heart she saw before her the very man for her hero. A woman's hero gives some censure, not of what she is, hardly of what she would like to be, but of what she would like to pass for. Here was the ideal for which Phemy had so long been waiting. She gazed up at him with a mixture of shyness and boldness not uncommon in persons of her silly kind, and Francis saw at once that she was an unusually pretty girl. He saw also that she was very prettily dressed, and, being one of those men who, imagining themselves gentlemen, feel at liberty to take liberties with women socially their inferiors, he plucked a narcissus from the edge of the path and said—at the same time taking the leave he asked—"Let me finish your dress by adding this to it! Have you got a pin?—There! All you needed to make you just perfect!"

Her face was now in a very flame. She saw he was right in the flower he had chosen, and he saw, not his artistic success only, but her recognition of it as well, and was gratified. He had a keen feeling of harmony in form and color, and flattered women, while he paraded his own insight, by bringing it to bear on their dress.

The flower in its new position seemed radiant with something of the same beauty in which it was set. But in truth there was more expression in the flower than was yet in the face. The flower expressed what God was thinking of when he made it; the face, what the girl was thinking of herself. When she ceased thinking of herself, then, like the flower, she would show what God was thinking of when he made her.

Francis, like the man he was, thought what a dainty little lady she would make if he had the making of her, and at once began talking as he never would have talked had she been what is conventionally called a lady—namely, with a familiarity to which their old acquaintance gave him no right, and which showed him not his sister's keeper. She, poor child, was pleased with his presumption, taking it for a sign that he regarded her as a lady. And from that moment her head at least was full of the young laird. She had forgotten all she came about.

When he turned and walked down the garden, she walked alongside of him like a linnet by a tall stork, who thought of her as a very pretty green frog. Lost in delight at his kindness, and yet more at his admiration, she felt as safe in his hands as if he had been her guardian angel. Had he not convinced her that her notion of herself was correct? Who should know better whether she was a lady, whether she was lovely or not, than this great, handsome, perfect gentleman? She accompanied him without hesitation into a little arbor at the bottom of the garden, and sat down with him on the bench there provided for the weary and the idle— in this case a soon-to-be gallant officer, bored to death by a week at home with his mother, and a girl who spent the most of her time in making, altering, and wearing her dresses.

"How good it was of you, Phemy," he said, "to come to see

me. I was ready to die for want of something pretty to look at. I was wondering how I had been able to live in this country so long. But suddenly the whole country is lovely from the light of your face."

"I am so glad," answered poor Phemy, hardly knowing what she said. It was to her the story of a sad gentleman who fell in love at first sight with a beautiful lady who was learning to love him through pity.

Her admiration of him was as clear as the red and white on her face, and foolish Francis felt in his turn flattered, for he too was fond of himself. There is no more pitiable sight to lovers of their kind than two persons falling into the love rooted in self-love. But possibly they are neither to be pitied nor laughed at; they may be plunging thus into a saving hell.

"You would like to make the world beautiful for me, Phemy?" rejoined Francis.

"I should like to make it a paradise," returned Phemy.

"A garden of Eden, and you the Eve in it?" suggested Francis.

Phemy could find no answer beyond a confused look and a yet deeper blush.

Talk elliptical followed, not unmingled with looks bold and shy. They had not many objects of thought in common, therefore not many subjects for conversation. There was no poetry in Gordon, and but the flimsiest sentiment in Phemy. Her mind was feebly active, his full of tedium. Hers was open to any temptation from him, and his to the temptations of usurping the government of the world, of thinking himself the benefactor of this innocent creature, and able to enrich her life with the bliss of loving a noble object. Of course he meant nothing serious! Equally of course would he do her no harm. To lose him would make her miserable for a while, but she would not die of love, and would have something to think about all her dull life afterward.

At length Phemy got frightened at the thought of being found with him, and together they went to look for her aunt. Finding her in a little outside building that was used for a laundry, Francis told Mrs. Bremner that they had been in the garden ever so long searching for her, and he was glad of the opportunity of hearing about his old friend, Phemy's father.

The aunt was not quite pleased, but said little.

The following Sunday Mrs. Bremner told the schoolmaster what had taken place, for of course Phemy would never so much have hinted at it to her father, and came home in a rage at the idiocy of a man who would not open his eyes when his house was on fire. It was all her sister's fault, she said, for having married such a book-idiot! She felt very uncomfortable about the two young people, and did her best in the way of warning. But Phemy seemed *so* incapable of understanding what ill could come of letting the young laird talk to her that Mrs. Bremner despaired of rousing in her any sense of danger. And having no authority over her, she was driven to silence for the present. She would have spoken to her mistress had she not plainly foreseen that it would be of no use, that she would either laugh, and say that young men must have their way, or that she would fly into a fury with Phemy for trying to entrap *her* son and with Mrs. Bremner for imagining that he would look at the hussy. One thing only was certain— that, if his mother opposed him, Francis would persist.

15 / A Novel Abduction

Phemy seldom went to the castle, but the young laird and she met pretty often. There was solitude enough in that country for an army of lovers. Once or twice Gordon came to take tea at her father's, and was cordially received by the schoolmaster, who had no sense of impropriety in their strolling out together afterward, leaving him well content with the company of his books.

Before this happened twice, all the town was talking about it, and predicting that no good could come of it. Phemy heard nothing and feared nothing. But if feeling had been weather and talk tempest, she would have been glad enough to stay inside. So rapidly, however, did the whirlwind of tongues extend its gyration that within half a week it reached Kirsty, and cast her into great perplexity of mind. Her poor silly, defenseless Phemy, the child of her friend the schoolmaster, was in danger from the son of her father's friend! Her father could do nothing, for Francis would not listen to him. Therefore, she thought, she must do something herself! She could not sit still and look on at the devil's work!

Having always been on terms of sacred intimacy with her mother, she knew more of the dangers of the world, while she was far safer from them, than such girls as their natural guardians watch instead of fortifying, and understood perfectly that an unwise man is not to be trusted with a foolish girl. She felt, therefore, that inaction on her part would be faithlessness to the teaching of her mother, as well as treachery to her father, whose friend's son was in peril of doing a fearful wrong to one to whom he owed almost a brother's protection for his schoolmaster's sake. She did not believe that Francis *meant* Phemy any harm, but she was certain he thought too much of himself ever to marry her; and were the poor child's feelings to count for nothing? She had no hope whatever that Phemy would listen to any sort of reasoning from her; but she must in fairness, before she *did* anything, try at least to have a talk with her.

She made repeated efforts to see her, but without success. She tried one time of the day, then another, then another; but, first by accident, then by clever contrivance, Phemy managed to keep out of her sight. She had of late grown tricky.

One of the windows of the schoolmaster's house commanded a view of the street in both directions, and Phemy commanded the window. When she saw Kirsty coming she would run into the garden and take refuge in the summerhouse, telling the servant on her way that she was going out and did not know when she would be back. On more occasions than one Kirsty said she would wait. Then Phemy, learning she was not gone, went out in earnest and made sure Kirsty had enough of waiting. Such shifts of cunning no doubt served laughter to the lovers when next they met, but they showed that Phemy was in some degree afraid of Kirsty.

Had Kirsty known the schoolmaster no better than his sister-in-law knew him, she would, like her, have gone to him. But she was perfectly certain that it would be almost impossible to rouse him. As it was, he turned a deaf ear and indignant heart to every one of the reports that reached him. To listen to them would be to doubt his child! Why should not the young laird fall in love with her? What more natural? Was she not worth as much honor as any man, be he who he might, could confer upon her? He cursed the gossips of the town, and returned to his books.

At length Kirsty was convinced that Phemy was avoiding her, and resolved to take her own way. And her way was a somewhat masterful one.

About a mile from Castle Weelset, in the direction of Tiltowie, the road was, for a few hundred yards, close-flanked by steep heathery braes. Now Kirsty had heard of Phemy's being seen several times on this road in recent weeks, and near the part of it I have just described, she resolved to waylay her. From the brae on the side next to Corbyknowe, she could see the road for some distance in either direction.

For a week she watched in vain. She saw the two pass together more than once, and she saw Francis pass alone, but she had never seen Phemy alone.

One morning, just as she arrived at her usual outlook, she saw Mrs. Bremner on the road below, coming from the castle, and ran down to speak to her. In the course of their conversation she learned that Francis was to leave for London the next morning. When they parted, the old woman resumed her walk to Tiltowie, and Kirsty climbed the brae and sat down in the heather. Now she was more anxious than ever. She had done her best but it had come to nothing, and now she had but one chance more. That Francis Gordon was going away so soon was good news, but what might still happen even before he went? She could think of nothing to do but keep watch as before, firm in her resolve to speak to Phemy alone, but now determined to speak to both if Francis was with her, and all but determined to speak to Francis alone if an opportunity of doing so should be given her.

All morning and afternoon she watched in vain. At last, in the evening—it was an evening in September, cold and clear, the sun down, and a melancholy glory hanging over the place of his vanishing—she saw the solitary form of Phemy hastening along the road in the direction of the castle. Although she had been looking out for her all day, at the moment she was so taken up with the sunset that Phemy was almost under where she stood before she saw her. She ran at full speed a hundred yards, then slid down a part of the brae too steep to climb, and leaped into the road a few feet in front of Phemy—so suddenly that the girl jumped with a cry and stopped. The moment she saw who it was, however, she drew herself up and would have passed with a stiff greeting. But Kirsty stood in front of her and would not permit her.

"What do you want, Kirsty Barclay?" demanded Phemy, who had within the last week or two advanced considerably in confidence of manner. "I am in a hurry."

"Ye're in a worse hurry than ye ken, for yer hurry should be in the other direction," answered Kirsty. "And I'm goin' to turn ye, or at least no let ye go wi'oot hearin' a bit o' the truth frae a woman older than yersel'. Lassie, ye seem to think naebody worth listenin' to a word frae except one man; but I mean ye to listen to me! Ye dinna ken what ye're aboot. I ken Francie Gordon a heap better than you, and though I ken nae ill o' him, I ken as little good. He never did naethin' yet but to please himsel', and there never came salvation or comfort to man, woman, or bairn frae any poor creature like *him*!"

"How dare you speak such lies of a gentleman behind his back!" cried Phemy, her eyes flashing. "He is a friend of mine and I will not hear him spoken of so."

"There's small harm can come to any man frae the truth, Phemy," answered Kirsty. "Set the man in front o' me and I'll say word for word to his face what I'm sayin' to you behind his back."

"Miss Barclay," rejoined Phemy, with a rather pitiable attempt at dignity, "I can permit no one to call me by my first name who speaks so ill of the man to whom I am engaged."

"That shall be as ye please, Miss Craig. But I would let you call me all the ill names in the dictionary to get ye to hearken to me! I'm tellin' ye naethin' but what's true as death."

"I call no one names. I am always civil to my neighbors whoever they may be. I will not listen to you."

"Oh, lassie. There's none o' yer neighbors that has a good word for what ye're doin'."

"Their lying tongues are nothing to me! I know what I am about! I will not stay a moment longer with you. I have an important engagement."

Once more, as several times already, she would have passed her, but Kirsty yet again stepped in front of her.

"I can weel take yer word," replied Kirsty, "that ye hae an engagement. But ye said a minute ago that ye was engaged to him: tell me in one word—has Francie Gordon promised to marry ye?"

"He has as good as asked me," answered Phemy, who had fits of apprehensive recoil from a downright lie.

"Noo there I could almost believe ye! Ay, that would be ill enough for Francie. He never was a doonright liar, sae long as I kenned him—any more than yersel'. But, for God's sake, Phemy, dinna imagine he'll ever marry ye, for that he will not."

"This is really insufferable!" cried Phemy, in a voice that began to tremble from the approach of angry tears. "Tell me, do *you* have a claim upon him?"

"Not even a shadow of one," returned Kirsty. "But my father and his father were like brothers, and we hae to do what we can for his father's son. I would fain try to keep him frae gettin' into trouble wi' you or any lass."

"I get him into trouble! Really, Miss Barclay, I do not know how to understand you!"

"I see I must be plain wi' ye. I wouldna hae ye get him into trouble by lettin' him get you into trouble!—and that's plain speakin'!"

"You insult me!" said Phemy.

"Ye drive me to speak plain!" answered Kirsty. "That lad, Francie Gordon—"

"Speak with respect of your superiors," interrupted Phemy.

"I'll speak wi' respect o' onybody I hae respect for!" answered Kirsty.

"Let me pass, you rude young woman!" cried Phemy, who had of late been cultivating in her imagination such speech as she thought would befit Mrs. Gordon of Castle Weelset.

"I winna let ye pass," answered Kirsty; "—that is, no till ye hear what I hae to say to ye."

"Then you must take the consequences!" rejoined Phemy, and, in the hope that her lover would prove within earshot, began a piercing scream.

It roused something in Kirsty that she could not afterward identify: she was sure it had nothing to do with anger. She felt, she said, as if she had to deal with a child who insisted on playing with fire beside a barrel of gunpowder. At the same time she did nothing but what she had beforehand, in case of the repulse she expected, resolved upon.

She caught up the little would-be lady as if she had been that same naughty child, and the suddenness of the action so astonished Phemy that for a moment or two she neither moved nor uttered a sound. The next, however, she began to shriek and struggle wildly as if she had been in the hug of a giant bear; whereupon Kirsty covered her mouth with one hand while she held her fast with the other. It was a violent proceeding, undoubtedly, but Kirsty chose to be thus far an offender, and yet farther.

Bearing her as she best could, she carried her toward Tiltowie until she reached a place where the road was bordered by a more practicable slope. Here she took to the moorland and made for Corbyknowe. Her resolve had been from the first, if Phemy would not listen, to carry her, like the unmanageable child she was, home to the mother whose voice had always been to herself the oracle of God. It was in a loving embrace, though hardly a comfortable one, and to a heart full of pity that she pressed the poor little runaway lamb. Her mother was God's vicar for all in trouble: she would he able to bring the child to reason. Her heart beating mightily with love and labor, Kirsty waded through the heather, hurrying along the moor.

It was a strange abduction. But Kirsty was divinely simple, and that way strange. Not until they were out of sight of the road did she set her down.

"Noo, Phemy," she said, panting as she spoke, "hold yer tongue like a good lassie, and come on with yer own feet."

Phemy took at once to her heels and her throat, and ran shrieking back toward the road, with Kirsty after her like a greyhound. Phemy had for some time given up struggling and trying to shriek, and was therefore in better breath than Kirsty, whose lungs were pumping hard. But Phemy had not a chance with her, for there was more muscle in one of Kirsty's legs than in Phemy's whole body. In a moment Kirsty had her in her arms again, and so tight that she could not even kick. Phemy gave way and burst into tears.

Kirsty relaxed her hold.

"What are ye gaein to do wi' me?" sobbed Phemy.

"I'm takin' ye to the best place I ken—home to my mither," answered Kirsty, striding on for home as straight as she could go.

"I winna go!" cried Phemy, whose Scotch had returned with her tears.

"Ye *are* goin'," returned Kirsty; "—at least I'm takin ye, and that's next best."

"What for? I never did ye an ill turn that I ken o'," said Phemy and burst afresh into tears of self-pity.

"Na, my bonny doo," answered Kirsty, "ye never did me any ill turn. It wasna in ye. But that's the less reason that I shouldna do you a good one. And yer father hae been sae good to me. It's no muckle I can do for you or him, but there's one thing I'm set upon, and that's keepin' ye frae Francie Gordon tonight. He'll be away tomorrow."

"Who telled ye that?" returned Phemy with a start.

"Yer ain aunt, honest woman," answered Kirsty. "And cryin' as she telled me, but it wasna at his leavin'."

"She might hae held the tongue o' her till he was gone! What was there to cry aboot?"

"Maybe she thought her sister's bairn in a trouble silence wouldna hide," answered Kirsty. "Ye haena a notion, lassie, what ye're doin' wi' yersel'. But my mither'll let ye ken, sae that ye winna go blin' into the foxhole."

"Ye dinna ken Frank, or ye wouldna speak o' him that way!"

"I ken him too weel to trust you to him."

"It's naethin' but ye're envious o' me, Kirsty, 'cause ye canna hae him yersel'. He would never look at a lass like you."

"It's weel everybody doesna see wi' the same eye, Phemy!

But for all that, I hae a whole side o' my heart soft to him: my father and his loved like brothers.''

"That canna be, Kirsty—and it's no like ye to lie. Yer father was a common soldier an' his was colonel o' the regiment.''

"True enough!'' replied Kirsty.

"Let me go, Kirsty! Please!'' said Phemy, taking herself again to entreaty. "I canna bide him to think I've played him false.''

"He'll play you false, whatever ye do or think. He'll no see ye tonight!''

Phemy uttered a childish howl, but immediately choked it with a proud sob.

"Ye're hurtin' me, Kirsty,'' she said after a minute or so of silence. "Let me doon and I'll go straight home to my father. I promise ye.''

"I'll set ye doon,'' answered Kirsty, "but ye must come home to my mither.''

"What'll my father think?''

"I'll not forget yer father,'' said Kirsty.

She sent out a strange, piercing cry, set Phemy down, took her hand in hers, and went on, Phemy making no resistance. In about three minutes there was a noise in the heather, and Snootie came rushing to Kirsty. A few moments more and Steenie lifted his cap to Phemy, and stood waiting for his sister's commands.

"Steenie,'' she said, "take the dog wi' ye, and run doon to the toon and tell Mr. Craig that Phemy here's comin' home wi' me to bide the night. Ye winna be longer than ye can help, and ye'll come to the hoose afore ye go up to the hill?''

"I'll do that, Kirsty. Come, doggie.''

Steenie never went to the town of his own accord, and Kirsty never liked him to go, for the boys were rude and made fun of him, but tonight it would be dark before he got there.

"Ye're surely not aboot to make me bide all night!'' wailed Phemy, beginning to cry again.

"I am that—the night, and maybe tomorrow night, and any

number o' nights till we're sure he's away," answered Kirsty, resuming her walk.

Phemy wept aloud, but did not try to escape.

"And he was gaein' to promise this very night that he would marry me!" she cried. But through her tears and sobs her words were indistinct.

Kirsty stopped and faced round to her.

"He promised to marry ye?" she asked.

"I didna say that. I said he was gaein to promise tonight. And noo he'll be gone, and never a word said!"

"He promised, did he, that he would promise tonight?—Eh, Francie, Francie! ye're no yer father's son! He promised to promise to marry ye! Eh, ye poor gowk o' a bonny lassie!"

"If I met him tonight—ay, it would come to that."

All Kirsty's inborn motherhood awoke. She clasped the silly thing in her arms, and cried out, "Poor wee dauty! If he hae a heart any bigger than the fox's, he'll come find ye to say sich a thing to ye—all the way to the Knowe if he hae to. Nae true man would be easily dissuaded o' sich an important thing!"

"He winna ken where I am!" answered Phemy, with an agonized burst of dry sobbing.

"Will he no? I'll see to that too—and this very night!" exclaimed Kirsty. "I'll give him the chance o' doin' the right thing."

"But he'll be angert at me!"

"What for? Did he tell ye no to tell?"

"Ay, he did."

"Worse and worse!" cried Kirsty indignantly. "He would try to get ye in his grip! He telled ye, nae doobt, that ye was the bonniest lassie that ever was seen, and praised ye sich as yer ain mither wouldna hae kenned ye. Jist tell me, Phemy, dinna ye think a hantle more o' yerself since he took ye in hand?"

She was trying to help Phemy to see that she had gathered from him no figs or grapes, only thorns and thistles. But such truths were beyond Phemy. She had been vain before, even without Francie's help.

Phemy made no reply. Did she not have every right to think well of herself? He had never said anything to her on that subject which she was not quite ready to believe.

Kirsty seemed to discern what was passing through her thoughts.

"A man that doesna tell ye the truth aboot himsel'," she said, "isna likely to tell ye the truth aboot *yersel'*! Did he tell ye hoo many lassies he had said the same thing to afore he came to you? It matters little sae long as they were lassies as heartless and empty-headed as himsel', and weel used to sich nonsense. But it's different wi' you, that never afore listened to sich and takes it a' for truth."

Phemy was not capable of following her. If she was lovely, as Frank told her, and as she saw herself in the mirror, why should she not be pleased with herself? If Kirsty had been made pretty like her, she would have been just as vain as she!

All her life the doll never saw the true beauty of the woman. Beside Phemy, Kirsty walked like an Olympian goddess. She was what she had to be, and never thought about it.

Phemy sank down in the heather, declaring she could go no farther. She looked so white and pitiful that Kirsty's heart filled again with compassion. Like the mother she was, she took the poor girl again in her arms, and, carrying her quite easily now that she did not struggle, walked with her straight into her mother's kitchen.

Mrs. Barclay sat darning the stocking that would have been Kirsty's affair had she not been stalking Phemy. Kirsty took it out of her mother's hands and laid the girl in her lap.

"Here's a new bairnie for ye, Mother!"

Kirsty sat on a stool nearby and went on with the darning.

Mistress Barclay looked down on Phemy with such a face of loving goodness that the poor miserable girl threw her arms round her neck and laid her head down on her shoulder. Instinctively the mother began to hush and soothe her, and in a moment more was singing a lullaby to her. Phemy fell fast asleep. Then Kirsty told what she had done; and while she spoke, the mother sat silent, brooding, and hushing, and thinking.

16 / Phemy's Champion

When she had told everything, Kirsty rose and laid aside the stocking.

"I must go to Weelset, Mother," she said. "I promised the girl I would let Francie ken whaur she was' and give him the chance o' sayin' his say to her."

"Very weel, lassie. Ye ken what ye're aboot, and I winna interfere wi' ye. But, eh, ye'll be tired afore ye get to bed."

"I'll take the gray mare."

"She's gey and fresh, lassie. Ye must be on yer guard."

"All the better," returned Kirsty. "To hear ye, Mother, a body would think I couldna ride!"

"Na. I weel ken yer father says there's no one in the countryside, man or woman, as takes to the beasts like yersel'. I'm jist exercising a mother's love to caution!"

When Kirsty entered the stable, the mare looked around and whinnied. Kirsty petted and stroked her, gave her two or three handfuls of oats, and while she was eating, strapped a cloth on her back. There was no sidesaddle about the farm. She could ride sideways on a man's, but she liked the way her father had taught her far better. Utterly fearless, she had, from his long years of training, grown to be a very capable horsewoman.

As soon as the mare had finished her oats, Kirsty bridled her, led her out, sprang on her back, and rode quietly out of the farmyard. The moment they were beyond the gate, she let her go. Almost the same moment the mare was away, up hill and down dale, almost at racing speed. So perfectly did Kirsty yield her lithe, strong body to every motion of the mare, abrupt or undulant, that neither ever felt a jar, and their movements seemed the outcome of a vital force common to the two. Kirsty never thought about whether she was riding well or ill, gracefully or otherwise, but the mare knew that all was right between them. Kirsty never touched the bridle except to moderate the mare's pace when she was too much excited to heed what Kirsty said to her. The whip she carried was one Colonel Gordon had given her father in remembrance of a little adventure they had had together, in which a lash from it in the dark night was mistaken for a sword cut, and did them no small service.

By the time they reached the castle, the moon was above the horizon. Kirsty brought the mare to a walk and rode gently up to the castle door.

A servant who happened to see her from the hall window saved her from having to ring the bell and greeted her respectfully, for everybody knew Corbyknowe's Kirsty. She told him she wanted to see Mr. Gordon, and suggested that perhaps he would be kind enough to speak to her at the door. The man went to find his master, and in a minute or two brought the message that Mr. Gordon would be with her presently. Kirsty drew back her mare into the shadow which, the moon being yet low, a great rock on the crest of the neighboring hill cast upon the approach. There she waited.

It was three minutes before Francis came sauntering round the corner of the house, his hands in his pockets and a cigar in his mouth. He gave a glance round, not seeing his visitor at once, and then, with a nod, came toward her, still smoking. His nonchalance, I believe, was forced and meant to cover uneasiness. For all that had passed to make him forget Kirsty, he yet remembered her uncomfortably, and at the present moment could not help regarding her as an angelic *bete noire*, of whom he was more afraid than of any other human being. He approached her in a sort of sidling stroll as if he had no actual business with her, but thought of just asking whether she would sell her horse. He did not speak, but Kirsty sat motionless until he was near enough for a low-voiced conversation.

"What are ye aboot wi' Phemy Craig, Francie?" she began, without a word of greeting.

Kirsty was one of those who pay little heed to the passage of time—with whom what was, is; what is, will be. She spoke to the tall, handsome man in the same tone and with the same forms as when they were boy and girl together.

He had meant their conversation to be at arms' length, so to speak, but his intention broke down at once, and he answered her in the same style.

"I ken naethin' aboot her. Why should I?" he answered.

"I ken ye dinna ken whaur she is, for I do," returned Kirsty. "Ye answered a question I never asked. What are ye aboot wi' Phemy, I challenge ye again. Poor lassie, she has no brother to defend her."

"That's all very well, but ye see, Kirsty," he began—then stopped, and having stared at her a moment in silence, exclaimed, "Lord, what a splendid woman you've grown into!"—He had probably been drinking with his mother.

Kirsty sat speechless, motionless, changeless as a soldier on guard. Gordon had to resume and finish his sentence.

"As I was going to say, *you* can't take the place of a brother to her, Kirsty, else I should know how to answer you. It's awkward when a lady takes you to task!" he added with a drawl.

"Dinna trouble yer head aboot that, Francie," rejoined Kirsty. Then changing to English as he had done, she went on: "I claim no consideration on account of not being a man."

Francis Gordon felt very uncomfortable. It was deuced hard to be bullied by a woman!

He stood silent because he had nothing to say.

"Do you mean to marry my Phemy?" asked Kirsty.

"Really, Miss Barclay," Francis began, but Kirsty interrupted him.

"Mr. Gordon," she said sternly, "be a man and answer me.

If you mean to marry her, say so, and go and tell her father—or my father, if you prefer. She is at the Knowe, miserable that she did not meet you tonight, poor child. That was my doing. She could not help herself."

Gordon broke into a strained laugh.

"Well, you've got her, and you can keep her," he said.

"You have not answered my question."

"Really, Miss Barclay, you must not be too hard on a man! Is a fellow not to speak to a woman but he must say at once whether or not he intends to marry her?"

"Answer my question."

"It is a ridiculous one!"

"You have been meeting with her in secret almost every night for something like a month," rejoined Kirsty, "and the question is not at all ridiculous."

"Then let the proper person ask me the question and I will answer it. But you have nothing to do with the matter."

"That is the answer of a coward," returned Kirsty. "You know yourself that you are taking advantage of the poor girl. You always were a fool, Francie, but now you are a wicked fool. If I were her brother—if I were a man, I would thrash you!"

"It's a good thing you're not able to, Kirsty. I should be frightened!" said Gordon, with a laugh and shrug, as if to throw the thing aside as done with.

"I said if I were a man," returned Kirsty. "I did not say, if I was able. I *am* able!"

"Very well," returned Francis angrily, "if you want to be treated as a man, I tell you I wouldn't marry the girl if the two of you went on your knees to me! A common, silly, country-bred flirt!—ready for anything a man—"

Kirsty's whip descended upon him with a merciless lash. The hiss of it, as it cut the air with all the force of her strong arm, startled her mare, and she sprang aside so that Kirsty, who had thrown the strength of her body into the blow, could not help but lose her seat. But it was only to land on her feet fronting her childhood friend. Gordon was grasping his head: the blow had for a moment blinded him. She gave him another stinging cut across the hands.

"That's frae yer father! The whip was his and I hae done for him what I could," she said, stepping back, as having fulfilled her mission.

He rushed at her with a sudden torrent of evil words. But he was no match for her in agility, as he might not have been in strength had she allowed him to close with her. But she avoided him as she had more than once a charging bull, every now and then dealing him another sharp blow from his father's whip. The treatment began to bring him to his senses.

"For God's sake, Kirsty!" he cried, ceasing his attempts to lay hold of her, "stop or we'll hae the whole hoose oot, and what'll come o' me then I darena think. I doobt I'll ever hear the last o' it as it is!"

"Am I to trust ye, Francie?"

"I winna lay a finger on ye, ye blasted fool!" he said in mingled wrath and humiliation.

Kirsty had been holding her mare by the bridle, and the horse had behaved as well as she could in the midst of the commotion. Just as Kirsty sprang on her back, the door opened and faces peered out. With another cut or two of the whip she encouraged a few wild gambols, so that all the trouble seemed to have been with the mare. Then she rode quietly through the gate.

Gordon stood in a motionless fury until he heard the soft thunder of the mare's hoofs on the turf as Kirsty rode home at a fierce gallop. Then he turned and went into the house, not to communicate what had taken place, but to lie about it as truthfully as he might find possible.

About halfway home, on the side of a hill across which a low wind—the long death-moan of autumn—blew with a hopeless wail among the heather, Kirsty broke into weeping. But before she reached home, all traces of her tears had vanished.

Gordon did not go the next day, nor the day after that, but he never saw Phemy again. It was a week before he showed himself at all, and then it was not a beautiful sight. He attributed the one visible wale on his cheek and temple to a blow from a twig as he ran in the dusk through the shrubbery after a strange dog. Even at the castle they did not know exactly when he left. His luggage was sent after him.

The domestics at least were perplexed as to the wale on his face until the man to whom Kirsty had spoken at the door hazarded a conjecture or two, which being not far from the truth, and as such accepted, the general admiration and respect that already were felt toward Corbyknowe's Kirsty were from that time forward mingled with a little wholesome fear.

When Kirsty told her father and mother what she had done at Castle Weelset, neither said a word. Her mother turned her head away, but the light in her father's eyes, had she had any doubt as to how they would take it, would have put her quite at ease.

17 / Francis Gordon's Champion

Poor little Phemy was in bed, and had cried herself asleep. Kirsty was more tired than she had ever been before. She went to bed at once, but for a long time was unable to sleep.

She did not repent of the chastisement she had given Gordon, yet the instant she lay down, back came the sudden something that had set her weeping on the hillside. The face of Francie Gordon, such as he was in their childhood, rose before her, but marred by her hand with stripes of disgrace from his father's whip. And with the vision came again the torrent of tears, for she realized that if his father had then struck him so, she would likely have been bold in Francie's defense. She pressed her face into the pillow lest her sobs should be heard. She was by no means a young woman ready to weep at anything. But the thought of the boy-face with her blows upon it got within her guard and ran her through the heart.

It is a sore thing when a woman, born a protector, has for protection to become an avenger. And Kirsty's revulsion from an act of violence foreign to the whole habit, though not inconsistent with the character of the calm, thoughtful woman, was severe. She had never struck even the one-horned cow that would, for very orneriness, kick over the milk pail. Hers was the wrath of the mother, whose very presence in a calm soul is its justification. The wrath was gone, and the mother soul turned against itself—not in judgment, but in irrepressible feeling. She did not for one moment think that she ought not to have done it, and she was glad in her heart to know that what she had said and she had done must keep Phemy and him apart. But there was the blow on the face of the boy she had loved, and there was the reflex wound in her own soul! Surely she loved him still with her mother-love, otherwise how could she have been angry enough with him to strike him!

For weeks the pain lasted keen, and was ever ready to return. It was a human type of the divine suffering in the discipline of the sinner, which with some of the old prophets takes the shape of God's repeating of the calamities he has brought on his people.

She could not tell her mother about it, and it was the only thing she ever kept from her. She could have told her father. For although she knew he was just as loving as her mother, he was not so soft-hearted and would not distress himself too much about an ache more or less in a heart that had done its duty. But as she could not tell her mother, she would not tell her father. But both parents saw that a change had passed upon her, and partially, if not altogether, understood the nature of it. They perceived that she had left behind her on that night a measure of her gaiety, that thereafter she was yet gentler to them, and if possible yet more tender to her brother.

For all the superiority constantly manifested by Kirsty in her relations with Francis, the feeling was never absent from her that he was of a race above her own. And now the sight of the young officer in her father's old regiment never could cross her mind's eye without the livid mark of her whip running from the temple down the cheek. But the face of the man never cost her a tear; it was only the scarred face of the boy that made her weep.

Another thing distressed her even more. The instant she had struck the first blow, she saw on his face an expression so meanly selfish that she felt as if she hated him. That expression had vanished from her visual memory; her whip had wiped it away. But she knew that for a moment she had all but hated him—if it was indeed *all but*.

All the house was careful the next morning that Phemy should not be disturbed; and when at length the poor girl appeared, looking as if all her color had been washed out by her tears, Kirsty made haste to get her a nice breakfast, and would answer none of her questions until she had eaten a proper meal.

"Noo, Kirsty," said Phemy at last, "ye must tell me what he said when ye let him ken that I couldna get to him 'cause ye wouldna let me."

"He didna say muckle to that. I dinna think he had been missin' ye."

"I see ye're no gaein to tell me the truth, Kirsty! I ken mysel' he must hae been missin' me dreadful!"

"Ye can judge nae man by yersel', Phemy. Men's different than lassies."

Phemy laughed superior.

"What ken ye aboot men, Kirsty? There never came a man near ye in the way o' wantin' to love ye."

"I'm no pretendin' to any experience," returned Kirsty. "I'm only talkin' aboot common sense. Is it likely, Phemy, that a man wi' grand relations and grand notions, wi' all manner of great ladies in his acquaintance . . . is it likely for sich a one, noo that he's an officer in the Company's service, to make a fool o' himsel' by bein as muckle taken up wi' a wee bit country lassie as she couldna help but be wi' him?"

"Noo, Kirsty, ye dinna need to try to make me mistrust one who's the very mirror o' all knightly courtesy," rejoined Phemy, speaking out of the high-flown, thin atmosphere she thought the region of poetry, "for ye canna! Naethin' onybody said could make me think different o' him."

"Nor naethin' he ever said himsel'?" asked Kirsty.

"Naethin'," answered Phemy, with strength and decision.

"No if it was that naethin' would ever make him marry ye?"

"That he might weel say, for he winna need makin'—but he never said it, and ye needna try to make me believe he did."

"He did say it, Phemy."

"Who telled ye? It's lies! Somebody's lyin'!"

"He said it to me himsel'. Never a lie hae onybody had a chance o' puttin' into the tale."

"He never said it, Kirsty!" cried Phemy, her cheeks now glowing, now pale.

"He wouldna dare!"

"He did dare, and he dared to *me*! He said, 'I wouldna marry her if both o' ye went doon on yer knees to me!' "

"Ye must hae angert him, Kirsty, or he wouldna hae said it. Of coorse he wasna to be guided by you. He *couldna* hae meant what he said! He would never hae said it to me! I wish I hadna let ye go to him. Ye hae ruined everything!"

"Ye never let me go, Phemy. It was my business to go."

"I see what's in it!" cried Phemy, bursting into tears. "Ye telled him hoo little ye thought o' me, and that made him change his mind!"

"Could he be worth cryin' aboot if that were the case, Phemy? But ye ken it wasna that. Ye ken that I wouldna do anything o' the sort. I'm ashamed even to deny it."

"Hoo am I to ken? There's no woman born but would fain hae him to hersel'!"

Kirsty held her peace.

"He didna say he hadna promised?" resumed Phemy through her sobs.

"We didna come to that."

"That's what I'm thinkin'."

"I dinna ken what ye're thinkin', Phemy."

"What did ye give him, Kirsty, when he told ye—no that I believe a word o' it!—that he would hae none o' me?"

"Jist a good lickin'," she answered.

"Ha, ha!" laughed Phemy hysterically. "I told ye ye was lyin'! Ye hae been naethin' but lyin', I ken that!—to make a fool o' me!"

For a moment despair overwhelmed Kirsty. Was it for this she had so wounded her own soul! How was she to make the poor girl understand? She lifted up her heart in silence. At last she said, "Ye winna see more o' him this year, I'm thinkin'. If ever ye get a scrap frae his pen, it'll surprise me. But if ever ye hae the chance, tell him I said I had given him his licks, and dare him to come and deny it to my face. He winna do that, Phemy. He kens too weel I would jist give him them again!"

"He would kill ye, Kirsty! *You* give him licks!"

"He might kill me, but he'd hae a part o' his licks first! And noo if ye dinna believe me, I winna talk no more aboot it. I hae been tellin' ye—no God's truth, it may be, but it's all true nonetheless. And it's no use, ye winna believe a word o' it!"

Phemy rose up like a pygmy fury.

"And ye laid hand to the cheek o' that kind o' man, Kirsty Barclay?—Lord, keep me frae killin' her!—Little holds me back frae tearin' ye to bits wi' my two hands!"

"I laid no hand on Francie Gordon, Phemy. I jist thrashed him wi' his ain father's ridin' whip, and my heart's like to break to think o' it. He'll probably carry the marks to his grave."

Kirsty broke into a convulsion of silent sobs and tears.

"Kirsty Barclay, ye're a devil!" cried Phemy in a hoarse whisper: she was spent with passion.

The little creature stood before Kirsty, her hands clenched and shaking with rage, blue flashes darting about in her eyes. Kirsty at once controlled the passion of her own heart, and sat still as a statue, regarding Phemy with a sad pity. A sparrow stood chattering at a big white brooding dove; and the dove sorrowed for the sparrow, but did not know how to help the fluttering thing.

"Lord!" cried Phemy, "I'll be cursin' all the world and God himsel' if I go on this way!—Eh, ye false woman!"

Kirsty jumped up, threw her arms around Phemy's so that she could not resist, and sat down with her on her lap.

"Phemy, if I was yer mither, I would give ye yer own licks for sayin' what ye didna in yer heart believe," she said. "All the time ye was keepin' company wi' Francie Gordon, ye ken in yer own soul ye was never right sure o' him. And noo I tell ye plainly that, although I struck him wi' my whip, I do not believe him so ill-contrived as ye would like me think him. Him and me was bairns together, and I ken his nature, and I take his part against ye, for, oot o' pride and ambition, ye're his own enemy: I do not believe ever he promised to marry ye. He's behaved ill enough wi'oot that—letting a gowk o' a lassie like ye believe what ye liked, and him only carryin' on wi' ye for the fun o' it 'cause he had naethin' to do. But a man's word's his word, and Francie's no sae ill as yer tale would make him! There, Phemy, I hae said my say!''

She loosened her arms. But Phemy lay still, and putting her arms round Kirsty's neck, wept in a bitter silence.

18 / Mutual Ministration _____

In a minute or so, the door opened and Steenie came into the kitchen one step, then stood and stared with such a face of concern that Kirsty had never seen on him before. I do not believe he had ever before seen a woman weeping. He shivered visibly.

"Phemy's not weel," said Kirsty. "Her heart's sae sore it makes her cry. She canna help it."

Phemy lifted her face from Kirsty's bosom and looked at Steenie with the most pitiful look countenance ever wore. Her rage had turned to self-commiseration. The cloud of mingled emotion and distress on Steenie's visage wavered, shifted, changed, and settled into the most divine look of pity and protection. Kirsty said she never saw anything so unmistakably godlike upon human countenance.

He turned away from them and stood for a time utterly motionless. Even Phemy was overpowered and stilled by that last look he cast upon her. After about three minutes he walked straight out of the house, not even turning to speak. Kirsty did not go after him: she feared to tread on holy ground uninvited. Nor would she leave Phemy until her mother came.

She got up, set Phemy on the chair, and began to get the midday meal, hoping Phemy would help her and gain some comfort from activity. And she was not disappointed. With a childish air of abstraction, Phemy rose and began, as of old in the house, to busy herself, and Kirsty felt much relieved. Phemy never spoke and went about her work mechanically. When at length Mrs. Barclay came into the kitchen, Kirsty thought it better to leave them together for a while, and went to find Steenie. She spent the rest of the day with him. Neither said a word about Phemy, but Steenie's countenance shone all the afternoon, and Kirsty left him at night in his house on the Horn, still in the afterglow of the meditation that had irradiated him in the morning.

When she came home, Kirsty found that her mother had put Phemy to bed. She had scarcely spoken all day, and seemed to have no life in her. In the evening, an attack of shivering with other symptoms showed that she was physically ill. Mrs. Barclay sent for her father, but the girl was asleep when he came. Aware that he would not listen to a word casting doubt on his daughter's discretion, and fearing that he might take her away to where she would not be so well cared for, Mrs. Barclay told him nothing of what had taken place. He thought her ailment would prove but a bad cold, and went back to his books without seeing her. Mrs. Barclay asked him to send the doctor, which he promised to do, but he never thought of it again.

Kirsty found her very feverish, breathing with difficulty and in considerable pain. She sat by her through the night, while Steenie was roving within sight of the window where the light was burning. He did not know that Phemy was ill; pity for her heartache drew him there. As soon as he thought his sister would be up in the morning, he went in: the door was never locked. She heard him, and came to him. The moment he learned Phemy's condition, he said he would go for the doctor, and left at once, taking a piece of oatcake in his hand for breakfast.

The doctor returned with him, and pronounced the attack pleurisy. Phemy did not seem to care what became of her. She was ill a long time, and for two weeks the doctor came every day.

There was now so much to be done that Kirsty could seldom go with Steenie to the hill. Nor did Steenie himself care to go up there for any long period of time, and he was never a night away from the house. When everyone was in bed, he would generally coil himself on a bench by the kitchen fire, ready at any moment to answer the lightest call from Kirsty, who took pains to make him feel himself useful, as indeed he was. Although now he slept considerably better at night and less in the day, he would start to his feet at the slightest sound, like the dog he had almost ceased to imagine himself except in his dreams.

Slowly, very slowly, Phemy recovered. But long before she was well, Steenie's family saw that the change for the better which had been evident in his mental condition for some time before Phemy's illness was now manifesting itself plainly in his person. The intense compassion that had been roused in his spirit seemed now settling in his looks and clarifying them. His eyes appeared to shine less from his brain and more from his mind. He stood more erect, and he gradually grew more naturally conscious of his body and its requirements. Coming upon him one morning, Kirsty saw him somewhat ruefully looking at his trousers. She suggested a new suit and was delighted to see his face shine up. He said he was ready to go with her and be measured for it.

In all these things she saw evident signs of a new start in the growth of his spiritual nature; and if she spied danger ahead, she knew that the God whose presence in him was making him grow was ahead with the danger also.

Steenie now not only began to go about attired as befitted David Barclay's son, but to an ordinary glance would have appeared in no way unusual. Kirsty ceased to look upon him with the pity that had till now colored all her devotion. Pride had taken its place, which she buttressed with a massive hope, for Kirsty was a splendid hoper.

People in the town, where Steenie was now seen oftener, would remark on the wonderful change in him. "What's come o' the fool Steenie?" said one of a group he had just passed. "Haith, he's lookin' almost like other fowk!"—"I'm thinkin' the devil must hae gone oot o' him," said another, and several joined in with their remarks.—"The muckle o' a devil was there to go oot! He was aye an unco harmless creature!"—"And that softhearted to a' livin' things!"—"Weel, the Lord takes care o' him, for he's one o' his own innocents!"

Before long Kirsty began to teach him to sit on a horse, and after a few weeks of her training he could ride pretty well.

It was many weeks before Phemy was fit to go home. Her father came to see her now and then, but not very often. He had his duties to attend to, and his books consoled him.

As soon as Phemy was able to leave her room, Steenie became her slave, and was ever after within her call. He seemed always to know when she would prefer him in sight and when she would rather be alone. He would sit for an hour at the other end of the room and watch her like a dog without moving. By this time Steenie could read a little, and his reading was by no means as fruitless as it was slow: he would sit reading, looking up every few moments to see if she wanted anything.

The girl became so accustomed to this mute attendance of love that she began to regard it as her right, and the spoiled little creature was given no occasion to imagine that it was not yielded her. And if at a rare moment she threw him a glance or small smile—a small crumb from her table to her dog—Steenie would for one joyous instant see into the seventh heaven, and all the day after dwell in the fifth or sixth. On fine, clear days she would occasionally walk a little way with him and Snootie, and then he would talk to her as he had never done except to Kirsty, telling her wonderful things about the dog and the sheep, the stars and the night, the clouds and the moon. But he never spoke to her of the bonny man. When on their return she would say they had a pleasant walk together, his delight would be unutterable. But all the time Steenie did not once venture a word belonging to any of the deeper thoughts in which his heart was most at home. Was it that in his own eyes he was but a worm glorified with the boon of serving an angel? Or was it that a sacred instinct of her incapacity for holy things kept him silent concerning such? At times he would look terribly sad, and the mood would last for hours.

Not once since she began to get better had Phemy alluded to her faithless lover. In its departure her illness seemed to have carried with it her unwholesome love for him, and she gradually became much more of a child. As her strength returned, she regained the childish merriment that had always drawn Kirsty, and the more strongly that she was not herself lighthearted. Kirsty's rare laugh was indeed a merry one, but when happiest of all she hardly smiled. Perhaps she never would laugh her own laugh until she opened her eyes in heaven. But how can anyone laugh his real best before that! Until then he does not even know his name.

Phemy seemed more pleased to see her father every time he came, and Kirsty began to hope she would tell him the trouble she had gone through. But then Kirsty had a perfect faith in her father, and a girl like Phemy never had. Her father, besides, had never been enough of a father to her. He had been invariably kind and trusting, but his books had been more to his moment-by-moment life than his daughter. He had never drawn her to him, never given her opportunity of coming really near him. No story, however, ends in this world. The first volume may have been very dull, and yet the next be full of delight.

19 / Steenie's Growth

It was the last week in November when the doctor himself came to take Phemy home to her father. The day was bright and blue, with a thin carpet of snow on the ground, beneath which the roads were in good condition. While she was getting ready, old David went out and talked to the doctor who would not go in, his wrinkled face full of light, and his heart glad with the same gladness as Kirsty's.

Mrs. Barclay and Kirsty busied themselves about Phemy, who was as playful and teasing as a pet kitten while they dressed her. But Steenie kept in the darkest corner, watching everything but offering no unneeded help. Without once looking or asking for him to say goodbye, never missing him in fact, with David's help Phemy climbed into the gig beside the doctor and began talking to him at once, never so much as turning her head as they drove away. The moment he heard the sound of the horse's hoofs, Steenie came quietly from the gloom and went out the back door, thinking no eye was upon him. But his sister's heart was never off him, and her eyes were oftener on him than he knew.

Lately he had begun again to go to the hill at night, and Kirsty feared his old trouble might be returning. Glad as she was to serve Phemy, and the father through the daughter, she was far from regretting her departure; for now she would have leisure for Steenie and her books once again, and now the family would gather itself once more into the perfect sphere to which drop and ocean alike desire to shape themselves.

"I thought ye would be after me!" cried Steenie as she opened the door of his burrow, within an hour of his leaving the house.

Kirsty had expected to find him full of grief because of Phemy's going, especially as the heartless girl had never even said goodbye to her most loving slave or given him a word of thanks. And she could see traces of emotion in his eyes, reminding her of lingering trouble as of a storm all but blown over. There was, however, in his face the light as of a far sunk aurora. She sat down beside him and waited for him to speak.

Never doubting she would follow him, he had already built up a good peat fire on the hearth, and placed for her beside it a low chair that his father had made for him and which he had himself covered with a sheepskin of thickest fleece. They sat silent for a while.

"Could ye say, Kirsty, that I was any use to her?" he asked at length.

"Ay, a heap," answered Kirsty. "I kenna what she would hae done wi'oot ye! She needed a heap o' lookin' after."

"And ye think maybe she'll be some the better for it?"

"Ay, I do think that, Steenie. But to tell the truth, I'm no sure she'll think very often aboot what ye did for her."

"Ow na! Why should she? There's no need for that. It was for hersel', no for her thinkin' aboot, that I tried. When I came in that day—the day after ye brought her home, ye ken—the look o' her poor, bonny face jist turned my heart ower in the middle o' me. Yon face o' hers comes back to me noo like the face o' a lost lammie that the shepherd didna think worth gaein' oot to look for. But if I hae a sore heart for her, the bonny man must hae sorer, and he'll do for her what he can. They call him the good shepherd, ye ken."

He sat silent for some minutes, and Kirsty's heart was too full to let her speak. She could only say to herself, "And fowk call him half-witted, do they. Weel, let them! If he be half-witted, the Lord's made up the other half wi' better!"

"Ay!" resumed Steenie. "The good shepherd loses no one o' them all! But I'll miss her dreadful! Eh, but I liked to watch the wan bit face grow and grow till it was round and rosy again. And eh, sich a bonny red and white it was! And noo she's back wi' her father, and it makes me happy to think o' it."

"Sae it makes me!" responded Kirsty, feeling, as she looked at him, like a glorified mother beholding her child walking in the truth.

"And noo," continued Steenie, "I'm right glad she's gone, and my mind'll be more at ease. For ye see, a week or two ago, I began to be troubled as I was never troubled afore. Afore she came I was most always thinkin' o' the bonny man. When my mind would grow dark, the face o' the bonny man would come to me and fill me up wi' the hope o' seein' him before long. But after she came, instead o' the face o' the bonny man would come up the face o' Phemy, and I didna like that, but I couldna help it. And a fear came to me that I was turnin' false to the bonny man. It wasna that I thought he would be vexed wi' me, but that I couldna bide anything to come atween me and him. Ye see, not bein' made altogither like other fowk, I couldna think aboot two things at once. So it troubled me to be thinkin' o' her all the time. Weel, today my heart was sore at her gaein' away. When she got into the doctor's gig and away they drove, my heart grew cold. But that very minute I heard, or was it jist as if I heard—I dinna mean with my ears, but in my heart, ye ken—a voice cry, 'Steenie, Steenie!' and I cried lood oot, 'Comin', Lord!' But I ken weel enough that the voice was inside me, and no in my head but in my heart—and nonetheless in me for that! So away at once I came to my closet here, and sat doon, and listened to the quiet o' my heart. Never a word came, but I grew quiet—eh, sae quiet and content. And I'm quiet yet. And as soon as it's dark, I'll go oot and see whether the bonny man be anywhere aboot. There's naethin' atween him and me noo."

"Steenie," said Kirsty, "it was the bonny man sent Phemy to ye—to give ye something to do for him, lookin' after one o' his silly lambs."

"Ay," returned Steenie, "I ken she wasna wiselike, sich as

you and my mither. She needed a heap o' lookin' after, as ye said."

"And wi' haein' to look after her, he kenned that the thoughts that troubled ye wouldna so weel get in, and would learn to stay oot. Jist look at ye noo!"

"I see it, Kirsty! I see it! I never thought o' the thing afore! I might be able to do a heap to make mysel' like other fowk! I winna forget, noo that I hae gotten a grip o' the thing! Ye'll see, Kirsty!"

"That's my ain Steenie," said Kirsty. "Maybe the bonny man couldna be comin' to ye himsel', and sae sent Phemy to let ye ken what he would hae o' ye. Noo that ye hae begun, ye'll be growin' more and more like other fowk."

"Eh, but ye fear me! I may grow ower like other fowk! I must get oot, Kirsty. I'm growin' afraid!"

"What for, Steenie?" cried Kirsty, not a little frightened herself, laying her hand on his arm. She feared his old trouble was returning in force.

" 'Cause other fowk never sees the bonny man, they tell me," he replied.

"That's their own fault," answered Kirsty. "They might all see him if they would—or at least hear him say they would see him afore long."

"Ay, but I'm no sure that ever I did see him, Kirsty!"

"That winna keep ye frae seein' him when the hour comes. And the same is true o' the rest."

"Ay, for I canna do wi'oot him—and sae neither can they."

"Naebody can."

"I hae as good as seen him, Kirsty! He was there! He helped me when the ill fowk came to pull at me! Do ye think, Kirsty, that I will see him someday?"

"I'm thinkin' the hour's been aye set for that for some time," answered Kirsty.

"Did ye ever hear tell that he had a father? I heard a man once say that he had. Sich a bonny man as that father must be! Jist think o' his haein' a son like *him*!—and him sich a man himsel'. Hoo can it be, Kirsty?"

"That'll be one o' the secrets the bonny man's gaein' to tell his ain fowk when he gets them home wi' him."

"His ain fowk, Kirsty?"

"Ay, sich as you and me. When we go home, he'll tell us all aboot a heap o' things we would fain ken."

"His ain fowk! His ain fowk!" Steenie went on murmuring to himself at intervals.

"What makes them his ain fowk, Kirsty?"

"What makes me yer fowk, Steenie?" she rejoined.

"That's easy to tell. It's 'cause we hae the same father and mither. I hae aye kenned that!" answered Steenie with a laugh.

He thought she had been trying to puzzle him, but had failed.

"Weel, the bonny man and you and me, we hae all the same father. He's the God who made the world and all o' us. And he's the bonny man's father too, though he helped him make the world. That's what makes us his ain fowk—ye see noo?"

"Ay, I see! I see!" responded Steenie, and again was silent.

Kirsty thought he now had plenty to meditate on.

"Are ye comin' home wi' me," she asked, "or are ye gaein' to bide the night?"

"I'll go home wi' ye, if ye like, but I would rather bide the night," he answered. "I'll hae jist this one night more oot upon the hill; and then in the mornin' I'll come home to the hoose and see if I can help my mither, or maybe my father. That's what the bonny man would like best, I'm sure."

Kirsty went home with a glad heart.

Surely Steenie was now in a fair way of becoming, as he phrased it, "like other fowk!"

"But the Lord's gowk is better than the world's prophet!" she said to herself.

20 / The Horn in Winter

The beginning of winter had been open and warm, and very little snow had fallen. This was much in Phemy's favor, and by the new year she was quite well. But, notwithstanding her indifference toward Steenie, she was no longer quite like her old self. She was quieter—and less foolish. She had a lesson in folly and a long ministration of love, and now knew a trifle about both. It is true she wrote nearly as much silly poetry, but it was not quite so silly as before, partly because her imagination had now something of fact to go on; and poorest fact is better than mere fancy. She even began to go of herself to see her aunt at the castle.

At Mrs. Bremner's request Phemy had made an appointment to go with her from the castle on a certain Saturday to visit a distant relative who lived in a lonely cottage on the other side of the Horn—a woman too old ever to leave her home. When the day arrived, both saw that the weather gave signs of breaking, but the heavy clouds on the horizon seemed no worse than had often shown themselves that winter, and such as often passed away. The air was warm, the day bright, the earth dry, and Phemy and her aunt were in good spirits. They had purposed to return early to Weelset, but agreed as they went that Phemy, the days being so short, should take the nearer path to Tiltowie over the Horn. Thus when their visit ended, they did not have such a great distance to walk together, Mrs. Bremner's way lying along the back of the hill, and Phemy's over the nearer shoulder of it.

As they took their leave of each other, a little later than they had intended, Mrs. Bremner cast a glance at the gathering clouds and said, "I dinna, doobt, lassie, it's gaein' to ding on afore the night! I wish we were home the two o' us. If it was to snow and blow both, we might hae ill gettin' there!"

"Naethin's to fear, Auntie," returned Phemy. "It's a heap too warm to snow. It may rain, I wouldna wonder, but there'll be nae snow."

"Weel, be careful. If there be a drop o' wet, ye must change every stitch the minute ye're in the hoose. Ye're no that stout yet."

"I'll be sure, Auntie," answered Phemy, and they parted.

Before Phemy got to the top of the hill-shoulder, which she had to cross by a path no better than a sheep track, the wind had turned to the north and was blowing keen, with gathering strength, from the regions of everlasting ice, bringing with it a cold terrible to be faced by such a slight creature as Phemy. And so rapidly did its force increase that in a few minutes she had to fight for every step she took. When at last she reached the top, which lay bare to the continuous torrent of fierce and fiercer rushes of the wind, her strength was already all but exhausted.

The wind brought up heavier and heavier snow clouds, and darkness with them, but before the snow even began to fall, Phemy was in an evil case—in worse case, indeed, than she could know. In those regions the weather is as much to be respected, if not feared, as any pack of wild beasts, yet so much easier to ignore until too late.

In a few minutes the tempest had blown all the energy out of her, and she sat down where there was not so much as a stone to shelter her. When she rose, afraid to sit any longer, she could no more see the track through the heather than she could tell in which direction to turn. She began to cry, but the wind did not heed her tears; it seemed determined to blow her away. And now came the snow, filling the wind faster and faster, until at length the frightful blasts had in them, perhaps, more bulk of blinding and dizzying snowflakes than of the air which drove them. They threatened between them to fix her there in a pillar of snow. It would have been terrible indeed for Phemy on that waste hillside, but the cold and the tempest quickly stupefied her.

Kirsty always enjoyed the winter heartily. For one thing, it roused her poetic faculty—oh, how different in its outcome from Phemy's!—far more than the summer. That very afternoon, leaving Steenie with his mother, she paid a visit to the Pict house; and there, in the heart of the earth, made up the following little song, addressed to the sky-soaring lark:

> What gars ye sing sae, birdie,
> As gien ye war lord o' the lift?
> On breid ye're an unco sma' lairdie,
> But in hicht ye've a kingly gift!
>
> A' ye hae to coont yersel' rich in,
> 'S a wee mawn o' glory-motes!
> The whilk to the throne ye're aye hitchin
> Wi' a lang tow o' sapphire notes!
>
> Ay, yer sang's the sang o' an angel
> For a sinfu' thrapple no meet,
> Like the pipes till a heavenly braingel
> Whaur they dance their herts intil their feet!
>
> But though ye canna behaud, birdie.
> Ye needna gar a'thing wheesht!
> I'm noucht but a hirplin herdie,
> But I hae a sang i' my breist!
>
> Len' me yer throat to sing throuw,
> Len' me yer wings to gang hie,
> And I'll sing ye a sang a laverock to cow,
> And for bliss to gar him dee!

Long before she had finished writing it, the world was dark outside. She had heard, but little heeded, the roaring of the wind over her. But when at length she put her head up out of the earth, it seized her by the hair as if it would drag it off. It took her more than an hour to get home.

In the meantime Steenie had been growing restless. Coming wind often affected him so. He had been out with his father, who expected a storm, to see that all was snug about byres and stables, and feed the few sheep in an out-building. Now he had come in, and was wandering about the house, when his mother prevailed upon him to sit down by the fireside with her. The clouds had gathered thick, and that afternoon was very dark, but all was as yet still.

He called his dog, and Snootie lay down at his feet, ready for what might come. Steenie sat on a stool, with his head on his mother's knee, and for a while seemed lost in thought. Then, without moving or looking up, he said, as if thinking aloud, "It must be fine fun up there among the cloods, afore the flakes begin to spread!"

"What do ye mean by that, Steenie, my man?" asked his mother.

"They must be packed sae close, like the feathers in a feather-bed, and then when they let them oot altogither, like holdin' the bed in their two hands by the bottom corners, they must be smotherin' thick till they begin to spread!"

"And who do ye think shakes oot the muckle flakes, Steenie?"

"I dinna ken. I hae thought aboot it often. I dinna think it's likely to be the angels. It's more like work for the bairnies up yonder, where every one, to the tiniest, kens what he's aboot and has somethin' to do. I would be surer, but that I hae thought sometimes I saw the muckle angels themsel's gaein aboot, through and through the heavy flutterin' o' the snow—no many o' them, ye ken, but jist sometimes one and sometimes another, through among the cold feathers, gaein' aye straight wi' their heads up, walkin' comfortable, as if they were at home in it. I'm thinkin' at sich a time they'll be after helpin' some poor body that the snow's likely to be ower muckle for. Eh me! If I could but get rid o' my feet and get up to see!"

"What for yer feet, Steenie? What ails ye at yer feet? Feet's gey useful kind o' things to creatures, whether they use two or four o' them."

"Ay, but mine's sich a weight! It's them that's aye been holdin' me doon! I would hae been up and away long since if it hadna been for them."

"And what would hae been comin' to us wi'oot ye, Steenie?"

"Ye would be doin' jist as weel wi'oot me that ye would be aye wantin' to be up and after me! A body's feet's nae doobt useful to hold a body steady, and keep him frae blowin' aboot, but eh, they're unco coombersome! But then they're unco good to hold a body frae thinkin' too muckle o' himsel'! They're fine humblin' things, a body's feet. But eh, it'll be fine wi'oot them!"

"Where on earth did ye get sich notions aboot yer feet? God kens there's naethin' amiss wi' yer feet! And ye hae nae reason to be ashamed o' them. The fact is, *yer* feet's unordinary small, Steenie, and canna add but unco little to yer weight."

"It's all that ye ken, Mother," answered Steenie with a smile. "But 'deed, I got my information aboot the feet o' fowk frae naethin' in this world. The bonny man himsel' sent word aboot them. He told the minister that told me once when I was at the kirk wi' ye, Mother—long, long ago—two or three hun'er years ago, I'm thinkin'. The bonny man told his ain fowk first that he was gaein' away in order that they mightna be able to do wi'oot him, and must stir themselves and come up after him. And then he slipped off his feet, and went up into the air where the snow comes frae. And ever since he comes and goes as he likes. And after that he told the minister to tell us we was to lay aside the weight that sae easy besits us and run. Noo by *run* he must hae meaned *run up*, for a body's no to run frae the devil but resist him. And what is it that holds onybody frae runnin' up the air but his feet? There!—But he's promised to help me off wi' my feet someday. Think o' that! Eh, if I could but hae my feet off! If they would but stick in my shoes. They're naethin' after all, ye ken, but the shoes o' my sowl!"

A gust of wind drove against the house and sank back just as suddenly.

"That'll be one o' them!" said Steenie, rising hastily. "He'll be wantin' me. It's no that often they want anythin' o' me besides the fair words all God's creatures look for frae one another, but sometimes they do want me, and I'm thinkin' they want me tonight. I must be gaein'."

"Hoots, laddie!" returned his mother. "What can they be wantin' o' ye? Sit doon and bide till they cry oot plain. I would fain hae ye safe in the hoose."

"It's all his hoose, Mother. Everythin' ootside's inside to him. He's safe in his ain hoose all the time, and I'm jist as safe atween his walls as atween yers. Didna naebody ever tell ye that, Mother? Weel, I ken it to be true. And for wantin' sich like as me, if God never hae need o' a mosquito, what for does he make sich a lot o' them?"

" 'Deed it's true enough ye say," returned his mother. "But I do wonder ye're never afraid."

"Afraid?" rejoined Steenie. "Why would I be afraid? What is there to be afraid o'? I never was afraid at face o' man or woman—na, nor beast neither!"

"Ah, but hearken to me: ye mustna go oot," said his mother anxiously. "If yer father and Kirsty would but come in to persuade ye! Thank the Lord that ye're no an orphan—that there's three o' us to take yer part."

"Naebody can be an orphan," said Steenie, "sae long as God's nae dead."

"Lord, and they call ye an idiot, do they!" exclaimed Marion Barclay. "—Weel, be ye or no, ye're one o' the babes in who's mouth he perfecteth praise!"

"He'll do that someday, maybe!" said Steenie.

"But, eh, Steenie," continued his mother, "ye winna go oot tonight?"

"Mother," he answered, "ye dinna ken, nor yet do I, what to make o' me—what wits I hae, and what wits I haena. But this ye'll allow, that for anythin' ye ken, the bonny man may be cryin' upon me to go after some poor little yowie o' his, oot alone in the storm and the night."

With these words he walked gently from the kitchen, his dog following him.

A terrible blast rushed right into the fire when he opened the door. But he shut it behind him easily, and his mother comforted herself that she had known him out in worse weather. Kirsty entered a moment after, and her father came in from the loft he called his workshop. They had their tea, and sat round the fire afterward, peacefully talking, a little troubled, but not particularly uneasy that their Steenie, the darling of them all, was away on the Horn. After all, he knew every foot of its sides better than the collie who, a moment ago asleep in front of the fire, was now following at his master's heels.

The wind, which had fallen immediately after the second gust as after the first, now began to blow with gathering force, and it took Steenie much longer than usual to make his way over height and hollow from his father's house to his own. But he was in no hurry, not knowing where he was wanted. I do not think he met any angels as he went, but it was a pleasure to think they might be about somewhere, for they were sorry for his heavy feet, and always greeted him kindly. Not that they ever spoke to him, he said, but they always made a friendly gesture—nodding a stately head, waving a strong hand, or sending him a waft of cool air as they went by, a waft that would come to him through the fiercest hurricane as well as through the stillest calm.

The snow had begun to fall before man and dog, strong toiling against the wind, reached their refuge among the rocks, and the night seemed solid with blackness. The very flakes might have been black as the snow of hell for any gleam they gave. But they arrived at last, and Steenie, making Snootie go in before him, entered the low door with bent head, and closed it behind them. The dog lay down weary, but Steenie set about lighting peat already piled between the great stones of the hearth. The wind howled over the waste hill in multitudinous whirls, and swept like a level cataract over the ghastly bog at its foot, but scarce a puff blew against the door of their burrow.

When his fire was well alight, Steenie seated himself on the sheepskin chair and fell into a reverie. How long he sat thus he did not know, when suddenly the wind fell, and with the lull both master and dog started together to their feet. Was it indeed a cry they had heard, or but a moan between wind and mountain?

The dog flew to the door with a whine and began to sniff and scratch at the crack of the threshold. Steenie, thinking it was still dark, went to get the lantern Kirsty had provided him with, but which he had never yet had occasion to use. The dog ran back to him and began jumping upon him, indicating that he wanted him to open the door.

A moment more and they were in the open universe, in a night all of snow, lighted by the wide swooning gleam of a hidden moon, whose radiance, almost absorbed, came filtering through miles of snow-cloud to reach the world. Nothing but snow was to be seen in heaven or earth, but for the present no more was falling. Steenie set the lighted lantern by the door, and followed Snootie, who went sniffing and snuffing about.

Steenie always regarded inferior animals, and especially dogs, as a lower sort of angels, with ways of their own, into which it would be time to inquire by and by, when either they could talk or he could bark intelligently and intelligibly—in which it used to annoy him that he had not yet succeeded. It was in part his intense desire to enter into the thoughts of his dog that used to make him imitate him the most of the day. I think he put his body as nearly into the shape of a dog's as he could in order thus to aid his mind in feeling as the dog was feeling.

As the dog seemed to have no scent of anything, Steenie thought for a moment what he should do, and then began to walk in a spiral, beginning from the door, with the house for the center. He had thus got out of the little valley onto the open hill, and the wind had begun to threaten reawakening when Snootie, who was a little way to one side of him, stopped short and began scratching like fury in the snow.

Steenie ran to him and dropped on his knees to help him. He had already got a part of something clear!

It was the arm of a woman. So deep was the snow over her that the cry he and the dog had heard could surely not have been uttered by her!

He was gently clearing the snow from the head, and the snow-like features were vaguely emerging, when the wind gave a wild howl, the night grew dark again, and in bellowing blackness the death-silent snow was upon them. But in a moment or two more, with Snootie's vigorous aid, Steenie had drawn the body of a slight, delicately formed woman out of its cold, white mold. Somehow, with difficulty, he got it on his back, the only way he could carry it, and staggered away with it toward his house.

Thus laden, he might never have found it, near as it was, for he was not very strong, and the ground was very rough as well as a little deep in the snow. But they had left such a recent track that the guidance of the dog was sure. The wise creature did not, however, follow the long track, but led pretty straight across the spiral for the hut.

The body grew heavy on poor Steenie's back, and the cold of it came through to his spine. It was so cold that it must be a dead thing, he thought. His breathing grew very short, compelling him to stop and rest several times. His legs became insensible under him, and his feet got heavier and heavier in the snow-filled, en-tangling, impeding heather.

He had always shrunk from death. Even a dead mouse he could not touch without a shudder. But this was a woman, and might come alive! It belonged to the bonny man, anyhow, and he would stay out with it all night rather than have it lie there alone in the snow. He would not be afraid of her, he was nearly dead himself, and the dead were not afraid of the dead. If she had only taken off her shoes! But she might be alive, and he must get her into the house! He would like to put off his feet, but most people would rather keep them on, and he must try to keep hers on for her!

With fast-failing energy he reached the door, staggered in, dropped his burden gently on his own soft heather bed, and fell exhausted.

He lay but a moment, came to himself, rose, and looked at the lovely thing he had labored to redeem from the cold. It lay just as it had fallen from his back, face upward.

It was Phemy.

For a moment his blood seemed to stand still. Then all the divine senses of the half-witted returned to him. There was no time to be sorrowful over her: he must serve the life that might yet be in the frozen form! He had nothing in the house except warmth, but warmth more than anything else was what the cold thing needed. With trembling hands he took off her half-thawed clothes, laid her in the thick blankets of his bed, and covered her with every woolen thing in the hut. Then he made up a large fire, in the hope that some of its heat might find her.

She showed no sign of life. Her eyes were fast shut: those who die of cold only sleep into a deeper sleep. Not a trace of suffering was to be seen on her countenance. Death alone—pure, calm, cold, and sweet—was there. But Steenie had never seen Death, and there was room for him to doubt and hope.

He laid one fold of a blanket over the lovely white face as he had seen a mother do with a sleeping infant, called his dog, made him lie down on her feet, and told him to watch. Then he turned away and went to the door. As he passed the fire, he coughed and grew faint. But recovering himself, he picked up his fallen stick, and set out for Corbyknowe and Kirsty.

Once more the wind had ceased, but the snow was still falling.

21 / Kirsty in the Storm

Kirsty woke suddenly out of a deep, dreamless sleep. A white face was bending over her—Steenie's—whiter than Kirsty had ever seen it. He was panting, and his eyes were huge. She jumped up.

"Come, come," was all he was able to say.

"What's the matter, Steenie?" she gasped.

For a quarter of a minute he stood panting, unable to speak.

"I'm no thinkin' anything's gone wrong," he faltered at length with an effort, recovering breath and speech a little. "The bonny man—"

He burst into tears and turned his head away. A vision of the white, lovely, motionless thing, whose hand had fallen from his like a lump of lead, lying alone at the top of the Horn, with the dog on her feet, had suddenly overwhelmed him.

Kirsty was distressed. She dreaded the worse when she saw him lose the self-restraint that had always till now been so remarkable in him. She leaned from her bed, threw her arms round him, and drew him to her. He kneeled, laid his head on her bosom, and wept as she had never known him to weep.

"I'll take care o' ye, Steenie, my man!" she murmured. "Ye've naethin' to fear." It is amazing how much, in the strength of its own power, love will dare to promise.

"Ay, Kirsty, I ken ye will, but it's no use," said Steenie.

He then gave a brief account of what had taken place.

"And noo that I hae telled ye," he added, "it all looks sae strange that maybe I hae been dreamin'. But it must be true, for

141

that must hae been what the angels came cryin' upon me for. I'm thinkin' they would hae brought me straight to her themsel's—they mostly gae aboot in twos—if it hadna been that the collie was equal to that."

Kirsty told him to go and rouse the kitchen fire and she would be with him in a minute. She sprang out of bed and dressed as fast as she could, thinking what would be best to take with her. "The poor lassie," she said to herself. In her heart she had little hope. It would be a sad day for the schoolmaster.

She went to her father and mother's room, found them awake, and told them Steenie's tale.

"It's time we were up, wuman!" said David.

"Ay," returned his wife, "but Kirsty canna bide for us. Ye must be off, lassie! Take a wee bit o' whiskey wi' ye, but mind, it's no that safe wi' frozen fowk. Hot milk's the best thing. Take a drappy o' that too, and I'll be up after ye wi' more. Dinna let Steenie gae back wi' ye. He canna be fit. Send him to me, and I'll persuade him."

"I'll saddle the mare and ride for the doctor," said David, making a motion to free himself from the covers. "I'll bring him straight to Steenie's hoose."

Kirsty went and got some milk to make it hot. But when she reached the kitchen, Steenie was not there, and the fire was all but black. The door of the house was open, and the storm drifting in. Steenie was gone back out into the night.

Hurriedly she poured the milk into a small bottle and thrust it into her bosom to grow warm as she went. She lit a lantern, mainly that Steenie might catch sight of it. Then she set out.

She started running, certain to overcome him, she thought. The wind was up again, but it was almost at her back, and the night was not absolutely dark, for the moon was somewhere. She was far stronger than Steenie, and could walk faster. But as keen as she looked out on all sides, before long she was near the top of the Horn and still had not caught a glimpse of him. The snow was falling, but not so thick that she could not see a good ways through it.

Could she have passed him? Or had he dropped on the way? One thing she was sure of—he could not have got to his house before her!

As she drew near the door she heard a short howl, and knew it for Snootie's. Perhaps Phemy had revived! But the cry of the dog was desolate and forsaken. The next moment came a glad bark. Was it the footstep of Kirsty it greeted, or the soul of Phemy?

With steady hand and a heart prepared for the worst, she opened the door and went in. The dog came bounding to her, then cringed at her feet, then stood wagging his tail.

Kirsty hesitated a moment; a weary sense of uselessness had overtaken her. But she cast off the oppression and followed the dog to the bedside. He jumped up and lay down where his master had placed him, as if to say he had been lying there all the time and had only got up the moment she came. It was the one warm spot in all the woolen pile. The feet beneath it were cold as the snow outside, and the lovely form lay motionless as a thing that would never move again. Kirsty lifted the blanket. There was Phemy's face, blind with the white death! It did not look at her, did not recognize her: Phemy was there and not there! Phemy was far away. Phemy could not move from where she lay!

Though seemingly hopeless, Kirsty tried her best to wake Phemy from her snow-sleep. But before long she gave up the useless task. She was thinking far more about Steenie than Phemy. But still he did not come.

"He must be safe back at home wi' Mother," she kept saying in her heart, but she could not reassure herself. While she was busy with the dead, he might be out some place slowly sinking into the same sleep from which she could not wake Phemy.

She left the snow-cold captive to sleep on. Calling the dog, she left the hut in the hope of meeting her mother, and learning that Steenie was at home.

Not until she opened the door of the hut had she any notion how fiercely the snow was now falling; neither until she left the hollow for the bare hillside did she realize how the wind was raging. Then indeed the world looked dangerous! If Steenie was out, if her mother had started, they were lost! She would have gone back into the hut with the dead except for the possibility that she might get home in time to prevent her mother from setting out, or might meet her on the way. At the same time the tempest between her and her home looked but a little less terrible to her than a sea breaking on a rocky shore.

22 / Kirsty's Dream

It was quite dark. Around Kirsty swept a whirlpool of snow. The swift flakes struck at her eyes and ears like a swarm of vicious flies. In such a wind, the blows of the soft thin snow, beating upon her face, now from one quarter, now from another, were enough to bewilder even a strong woman like Kirsty.

After trying for a while to force her way, she suddenly became aware of utter ignorance as to the direction in which she was going, and for the first time in her life a terror possessed her—not for herself, but for Steenie and her father and mother. All she could think was that they would go on looking for her till they too died, and all were buried yards deep under the snow!

She kept struggling on, her head bent and her body leaning forward, forcing herself against the snow-filled wind—but in which direction, she didn't know. It was only by the feel of the earth under her feet that she could tell, and at times she was by no means sure whether she was going up or down hill. She kept on and on, almost hopeless of getting anywhere, certain of nothing but that if once she sat down, she would never rise again. Fatigue that must not yield and the inroads of the cold sleep at length affected her brain, and her imagination began to take its own way with her. She thought herself condemned to one of those awful dust towers, a specially devilish invention of the Persians, in which the lungs of a culprit were at length absolutely choked up by the constant stirring of the dust to fill the air. Dead of the dust, she revived to the snow: it was fearfully white, for it was all dead faces. She crushed and waded through those that fell;

white multitudes came whirling up on her from all sides. Gladly would she have thrown herself down among them, but she must walk—walk on forever.

All the time she felt in her dim suffering as if not she but those at home suffered. She had deserted them in trouble, and do what she might—she would never get back to them!

Where was the dog? He had left her! He was nowhere near her! She tried to call him, but the storm choked every sound in her very throat. He would never have left her to save himself! He who makes the dogs must be at least as faithful as they!

Then she heard, or thought she heard the church bell, and that may have had something to do with the strange dream out of which she came gradually to herself.

Her dream was this:

She sat at the communion table in her own parish church, with many others, none of whom she knew. A man with piercing eyes went along the table, examining the faces of all to see if they were fit to partake. When he came to Kirsty, he looked at her for a moment sharply, then said, "That woman is dead. She has been in the snow all night. Lay her in the vault under the church."

She rose to go because she was dead, and hands were laid upon her to guide her as she went.

They brought her out of the church into the snow and wind, then turned away to leave her. But she remonstrated, "The man with the eyes," she said, "gave the order that I should be taken to the vault of the church."

"Very well," answered a voice, "there is the vault, creep into it!"

She saw an opening in the ground, at the foot of the wall of the church, and getting down on her hands and knees, she crept through it, and with difficulty got into the vault. There, all was still. She heard the wind raving, but it sounded far off. Who had guided her there? One of Steenie's storm-angels, or the Shepherd of the sheep? It was all the same, for the storm-angels were his sheep dogs. She had been bewildered by the terrible beating of the snow-wind, but her own wandering was another's guiding! Beyond the turmoil of life and unutterably happy, she fell asleep, and the dream left her. In a little while, however, it came again.

She was lying, she thought, on the stone floor of the church vault, and wondered whether the examiner, notwithstanding the shining of his eyes, might not have made a mistake. Perhaps she was not so very dead! Perhaps she was not quite unfit to eat of the bread of life, after all! She moved herself a little, then tried to rise, but failed; tried again, and again, and at last succeeded.

All was dark around her, but something seemed present that was known to her—whether man or woman or beast or thing, she could not tell. At last she recognized it; a familiar odor it was, a peculiar smell, of the kind we call earthy. It was the air of her own earth house, in days that seemed far away. Perhaps she was in it now! Then her box of matches might be there too! She felt about and found it. With trembling hands she struck one and proceeded to light her lamp.

It lit up. Something seized her by the heart.

A little farther in, stretched on the floor, lay a human form on its face. She knew at once that it was Steenie's. The feet were toward her, and between her and them a pair of shoes: he was dead! He had got rid of his feet at last!—he was gone after Phemy—gone to the bonny man.

She knelt and turned the body over. Her heart was like a stone. She raised his head on her arm: it was plain he was dead. A small stream of blood had flowed from his mouth and made a little pool, not yet quite frozen.

Kirsty's heart was about to break from her bosom to go after him.

Then the eternal seemed to descend upon her like a waking sleep, a clear consciousness of peace. It was for a moment as if she saw the Father at the heart of the universe, with all his children about his knees. Her pain and sorrow and weakness were suddenly gone. She wept glad tears over the brother called so soon from the nursery to the great presence chamber.

"Ah, bonny man!" she cried, "is it possible to expect too muckle frae yer father and mine?"

She sat down beside what was left of Steenie, and ate of the oatcake and drank of the milk she had carried, forgotten until now.

"I wonder what God'll do wi' the two o' them," she said to herself. "If I loved them both as I did, *he* loves them better!"

She rose and went out.

Light had come at last, but too dim to be more than gray. The world was one large white sepulchre in which the earth lay dead. Warmth and hope and spring seemed gone forever. But God was alive; his hearth fire burned; therefore death was nowhere. She knew it in her own soul, for the Father was there, and she knew that in his heart were all the loved.

The wind had ceased, but the snow was still falling, here and there a flake. A faint blueness filled the air, and was colder than the white. Whether the day was at hand or the night, she could not distinguish. The church bell began to ring, sounding from far away through the silence. What mountains of snow must yet tower unfallen in the heavens, when it was nearly noon and still so dark! But Steenie was out of the snow—that was well! Or perhaps he was beside her in it; only, he could leave it when he would! Surely Phemy must be with him! For who knows what she might have been thinking during that last cold walk? She could not be left all alone and so silly! And Steenie, no doubt, would have her to teach! His trouble must have gone the moment he died, but Phemy would have to find out further what a goose she was! Kirsty's thoughts cut their own channels: she was as far ahead of her church as the woman of Samaria was ahead of the high priest at Jerusalem.

Thus thinking, she kept on walking through the snow to find her mother and weep on her bosom. Suddenly she remembered and stood still: her mother was going to follow her to Steenie's house! She too must be dead in the snow!—Well, let heaven take them all! They were born to die, and it was her turn now to follow her mother! She started again for home, and at length drew near the house.

It was more like a tomb than a house. The door looked as if no one had gone in there or out for ages. Was this still only a dream? Would she find her father and mother but not be able to speak to them through her sleep? But God was not dead, and while God lived she was not alone even in a dream.

A dark bundle lay on the doorstep: it was Snootie. He had been scratching and whining until despair came upon him, and he lay down to die.

She lifted the latch, stepped over the dog, and entered. The peat fire was smoldering low on the hearth. She sat down and closed her eyes. When she opened them, there lay Snootie, stretched out before the fire. She rose and shut the door, fed and roused the fire, and brought the dog some milk, which he lapped up eagerly.

Not a sound was in the house. She went all through it. Neither her father nor mother was there. It was Sunday, and all the men of the farm were away. A cow lowed, and in her heart Kirsty blessed her: she was a live creature. She would go and milk her!

23 / How David Fared

David Barclay got up the moment Kirsty was out of the room, dressed himself in haste, swallowed a glass of whiskey, saddled the gray mare, gave her a feed of oats, which she ate the faster that she felt the saddle, and set out for Tiltowie to get the doctor.

Threatening as the weather was, he was well on the road before the wind became so full of snow as to cause him any anxiety either for those on the hill or for himself. But after the first moment of anxiety, a very few minutes convinced him that a battle with the elements was at hand more dangerous than he had ever had to fight with armed men.

For some distance the road was safe enough as yet, for the storm had not had time to heap up the snow between the bordering hills. But by and by he must come out upon a large field recovered by slow degrees and great labor from the bog. And there he would be exposed to the full force of the now furious wind, and in many places it would be far easier to wander off than to stay upon a road level with the fields, and bounded not even by a ditch the size of a wheel track.

When he reached the open, therefore, he was compelled to proceed at a slow walking pace through the thick, blinding, bewildering, tempest-driven snow. Nor was he surprised when, in spite of all his caution, he found by the sudden sinking and withdrawing of one of the mare's legs with a squelching noise that he had got astray upon the bog and did not any longer know in what direction the town or any other abode of humanity lay. The only thing he did know was the side of the road to which he had turned,

150

and that he knew only by the ground into which he had got: no step farther must be attempted in that direction! His mare seemed to know this as well as himself, for when she had pulled her leg out, she drew back a pace, and stood. David cast a knot on the reins, threw them on her neck, and told her to go where she pleased. She turned half round and started at once, feeling her way at first very carefully. Then she walked slowly on, with her head hanging low. Again and again she stopped and snuffed, diverged a little, and went on.

The wind was packed rather than charged with snow. Men said there never was a wind of that strength with so much snow in it. David began to despair of ever finding the road again, and naturally in such straits thought how much worse would Kirsty and Steenie be faring on the open hillside. He knew his wife could not have started before the storm rose to tempest, and would delay her departure.

Then he began to reflect how little at any time a father could do for the well-being of his children. The fact of their being children implied their need of an all-powerful father. Therefore, must there not be such a father? And with the question the truth dawned upon him, that first of all truths, which all his church-going and Bible-reading had till then failed to disclose, that, for life to be a good thing and worth living, a man must be the child of a perfect father and know him. In his terrible anxiety about his own children, he lifted up his heart—not to the Governor of the world, not to the God of Abraham or Moses, not to the God of the Church, least of all to the God of the Shorter Catechism, but to the faithful creator and Father of David Barclay. The aching soul, which none but a perfect father could have created capable of deploring its own father imperfection, cried out to the Father of fathers on behalf of his children; and as he cried, a peace came stealing over him such as he had never before felt.

Then he knew that his mare had for some time been going on hard ground, and was going with purpose in her gentle trot. In five minutes more, he saw the glimmer of light through the snow.

Near as it was, or he could not have seen it, he failed repeatedly in finding his way to it. The mare at length fell over a stone wall out of sight in the snow, and when they got up they found themselves in a little garden at the end of a farmhouse.

Not, however, until the farmer came to the door, wondering who could possibly be their visitor on such a morning as this, did he know to what farm the mare had brought him. Weary, and well aware that no doctor in his senses would set out for the top of the Horn in such a tempest of black and white, he gratefully accepted the shelter and refreshment which his mare and he found in this time of much need, and waited for a lull in the storm.

24 / How Marion Fared

In the meantime the mother of the family, not herself at the moment in danger, began to suffer the most. It dismayed her to find, when she came downstairs, that Steenie had, as she thought, insisted on accompanying Kirsty. But it was without any great anxiety that she set about preparing food with which to follow them.

She was bending over her fire, busy with her cooking, when all at once the wind came rushing straight down the chimney, blew sleet into the kitchen, blew soot into the pot, and nearly put out the fire. It was but a small whirlwind, however, and presently passed.

She went to the door, opened it a little way, and peeped out: the morning was a chaos of blackness and snow and wind. She had been born and brought up in a yet wilder region of the Highlands, but the storm threatened to be such as in her experience was unparalleled.

"God preserve us!" cried the poor woman. "Can this be the end o' all things? Is the earth turnin' into a muckle snow wreath that when all are dead, there may be nae fowk necessary to bury them? Eh, sich a grave! Mortal wuman couldna carry a basket in sich a snow! Losh, she wouldna carry hersel' far! I must bide a bit if I would be any help to them! It's my basket they'll be wantin', no me; and in this drift, basket may flee, but it winna float!"

She turned to her cooking as if it were the one thing to save the world. Let her be prepared for the best as well as for the worst!

Kirsty might find Phemy past helping, and bring Steenie home! Then there was David, at that moment fighting for his life, per- haps—if he came home now, or any of the three, she must be ready to save their lives! they must not perish on her hands!

So she prepared for the possible future, not by brooding on it, but by doing the work of the present. She cooked and cooked until there was nothing more to be done in that way, and then having thus cleared the way for it, sat down and cried. There was a time for tears. The Bible said there was, and when Marion's hands fell into her lap, their hour—and not till then, was come. To go out after Kirsty would have been the bare foolishness of suicide, would have been to abandon her husband and children against the hour of their coming need. One of the hardest demands on the obedience of faith is to do nothing; it is often so much easier to do something foolishly!

But she did not weep long. A moment more and she was up and at work again, hanging the great kettle of water on the crook and blowing up the fire so that she might have hot bottles to lay in every bed. Then she assailed the peat stack outside, in spite of the wind, making journey after journey to it, until she had heaped a great pile of peat in the corner nearest the hearth.

The morning wore on.

The storm continued raging. No news came from the white world. Mankind had vanished in the whirling snow. It was well the men had gone home, she thought. Had they been present, there would only have been the more danger. They would surely have gone out searching, and then all would have been abroad in the drifts of snow, hopelessly looking about for one another. But oh, Steenie, Steenie! and her own Kirsty!

About half past ten o'clock, the wind began to lessen in its violence, and then quickly sank to a calm. The snow soon lost its terror.

Marion looked out: it was falling in straight, silent lines, flick- ering slowly down, but very thick. She could find her way now!

Hideous fears assailed her, but she banished them imperiously: they should not sap the energy whose every tiniest bit would be needed! She caught up the bottle of hot milk she had kept ready, wrapped it in flannel, tied it together with a loaf of bread in a shawl about her waist, made up the fire, closed the door, and set out for Steenie's house on the Horn.

25 / Husband and Wife

Two hours or so earlier, David had perceived some abatement in the storm. His host offered to go at once to the doctor and the schoolmaster. Therefore, David had taken his mare and mounted to go home. He met with no difficulty now except for the depth of the snow, which made it hard for the mare to get along. Full of anxiety about his children, he found the distance a weary one to traverse indeed.

When at length he reached the Knowe, no one was there to welcome him. He saw, however, by the fire and the food, that Marion had not been gone long. He put up the gray mare, clothed her with a blanket and fed her, drank some milk, grabbed a quarter panfull of oatcakes, and started for the hill.

The snow was not falling so thickly now, but it had already almost obliterated the footprints of his wife. Still he could distinguish them in places, and with some difficulty succeeded in following their track until it was clear which route she had taken. They indicated the easier, though longer way—not that by the earth house, and the father and daughter passed without seeing each other. When Kirsty got to the farm, her father was following her mother up the hill.

When David reached the Hillfauld, the name he always gave Steenie's house, he found the door open, and walked in. His wife did not hear him, for his iron-shod shoes were balled with snow. She was standing over the body of Phemy, looking down on the white sleep with a solemn, motherly, tearless face. She turned as he drew near, and the pair, like the lovers they were, fell each in

156

the other's arms. Marion was the first to speak.

"Oh, David! God be praised that I hae yersel'!"

"Is the poor thing gone?" asked her husband in an awe-hushed tone, looking down on the maid.

"I doobt there's nae doobt aboot that," answered Marion. "Steenie, I was jist thinkin', would be sore disappointed to learn if there was. Eh, the faith o' that laddie! Heaven's to him sich a real place, and sich a hantle better than this world that he would not only fain be there himsel' but would hae Phemy there—ay, if it were ever sae long afore himsel'! Ye see, he doesna understand that Phemy was aye a considerably selfish kind o' lassie!"

"Maybe the bonny man, as Steenie calls him," returned David, "hae as muckle compassion for the poor thing in his heart as Steenie himsel'!"

"Ow ay! But what can the bonny man himsel' do, all bein' settled noo?"

"Dinna limit the Almighty, wuman. The Lord o' mercy'll manage to look after the lammie he made, one way or other, there as here. Ye darena say he didna do his best for her here, and will he no do his best for her there as weel?"

"Doobtless, David! But ye frighten me! It sounds jist like papistry—neither more nor less—to talk aboot God doing somethin' for her after she's sae dead. What *can* he do? He canna die again for one that wouldna turn to him in this life? The thing's no to be thought!"

"Hoo ken ye that? Ye hae jist thought it yersel'! If I was you, I wouldna dare to say what the Lord couldna do! There's too many fowks already doin' that, sayin' the Lord's atonement canna go beyond what they canna see wi' their own earth-bound eyes. We canna ken Phemy's heart, noo, can we? In the meantime, what he makes me able to hope, I'm no gaein' to fling frae me!"

David was a true man. He could not believe a thing with one half of his mind and care nothing about it with the other. He, like his Steenie, believed in the bonny man about in the world, not in the mere image of him standing in the precious shrine of the New

Testament. The Gospels were to him *life*, not mere past history to be read and analyzed and placed on his mental shelf of inactivity.

After a brief silence he asked, "Whaur's Kirsty and Steenie?"

"The Lord kens. I dinna."

"They'll be safe enough."

"It's no likely."

And therewith, by the side of the dead, he imparted to his wife the thoughts that drove misery from his heart when he sat on his mare in the storm with the reins on her neck, not even knowing where she went.

"Ay, ay," returned his wife after a pause, "ye're unco right, David, as ye always are! And I'm jist conscience-stricken to think hoo often I'm ready to mourn over the sorrow in *my* heart, never thinkin' o' the gladness in God's. What call had I to cry over Steenie when God must hae been aye pleased wi' him? Hoo can we lament when God's industriously settin' all things right? And eh, glad sure he must be wi' sich a lot o' his bairns as he has at home aboot him."

"Ay," returned David with a sigh, thinking of his old comrade and the son he had left behind him. "But there's the prodigal ones!"

"Thank God we hae nae prodigal!"

"Ay, thank him," rejoined David. "But he has prodigals that trouble him sore, and we must see to it that we're no thankless auld prodigals oorsel's."

Again followed a brief silence.

"Oh, but isna it strange?" said Marion. "Here we are mournin' over another man's bairn, and naewise kennin' what's come o' oor ain two! David, what *can* hae come o' Steenie and Kirsty?"

"The will o' God's what's come o' them. And God give me the grace to keep frae wishin' anythin' other than that for them."

"Weel, let's be away home and see whether the two hae been there afore us!— Eh, but the sight o' the bonny corpse must hae given Steenie a sore heart!"

"But what'll we do aboot it afore we go? The storm may come on again worse than ever and make it impossible to bury her for a month."

"We couldna carry her home atween us, David—do ye think?"

"Na, na. It's no as if it was hersel'. And cold's a fine keeper—better than the embalmin' o' the Egyptians! Only I dinna want Steenie to see her again."

"Weel, let's cover her in the bonny white snow!" said Marion. "She'll keep there as long as the snow keeps, and naethin'll disturb her till the time comes to lay her away."

"That's weel thought o'," answered David. "Eh, but it's a bonny burial compared wi' sich as I hae often given comrade and foe alike."

They went out and chose a spot close by the house where the snow lay deep. There they made a hollow and pressed the bottom of it down hard. They carried out and laid in it the death-frozen dove, and heaped upon her a firm, white, marble-like tomb of heavenly new-fallen snow.

Without reentering it, they closed the door of Steenie's refuge, and, leaving the two deserted houses side by side, made what slow haste they could, with anxious hearts, to their home. The snow was falling softly, for the wind was still asleep.

26 / David, Marion, Kirsty, Snootie, and What Was Left of Steenie

Kirsty saw their shadows darken the wall, and turning from her work at the dresser, ran to the door to meet them.

"God be thanked!" cried David.

Marion gave her daughter one loving look, and entering cast a fearful, questioning glance around the kitchen.

"Whaur's Steenie?" she said.

"He *must* be wi' Phemy, I'm thinkin'," faltered Kirsty.

"Lassie, are ye demented?" her mother almost screamed. "We're only this minute come frae there."

"He *must* be wi' Phemy, Mother. The Lord canna surely hae parted them, goin' in almost holdin' hands."

Marion sank on a chair and covered her face with her hands.

"The will o' God's accountable for him," said David, sitting down beside her, and laying hold of her arm.

She burst into terrible weeping.

"He must be happy at home wi' the bonny man!" said Kirsty.

"Lassie," said David, "you and me and yer mither, we hae naethin' left but to be better bairns, and go the faster to the bonny man. Whaur's what's left o' the laddie, Kirsty?"

"Lyin' in my hoose, as he called it. Mine was in the earth, his in the air, he said. He was away afore I got to the kitchen. He had jist killed himsel' wi' tryin' to save Phemy, runnin' and fetchin', on the barest chance o' savin' her life. And sae when he set off to go to her, no waitin' for me, he was so exhausted that he had a blood-break in his chest, and was jist able, and nae more, to creep into the earth hoose oot o' the snow. He didna like the place, and yet had a kind o' a notion o' the bonny man bein' there sometimes. I'm thinkin' Snootie must hae got to him and run home for help, for I found him almost dead upon the doorstep."

David stooped and patted the dog.

"Na, that couldna be," he said, "or he would never hae left him, I'm thinkin'. Ye're a braw dog," he went on to the collie, "and I'm thankful ye're no lyin' wi' yer tongue hangin' oot! Good comes to good doggies!" he added, petting the creature, who had risen and feebly set his paws on David's knees.

"And ye left him lyin' there!" sobbed the mother.

"Mother," said Kirsty, "he was better off than any o' the rest o' us! I winna say that I loved him sae weel as you, and I darena say I loved him as the bonny man loves his brothers and sisters. But I hae yet to learn hoo to love him better. Anyway, the bonny man wanted him, and he has him. And when I left him there, it was jist as if I held him oot in my arms and said, 'Here, Lord, take him: he's yer own.' "

"Ye're in the right, Kirsty, my bonny bairn," said David. "Yer mither and me was never but pleased wi' anything ye ever did—isna that true, Marion?"

"True as his word," answered the mother, and rose and went to her room.

David went out into the yard, saw that all was right with the beasts, and fed them. Then he made his way to his workshop over the cart shed, where in five minutes he constructed, with two poles run through two sacks, a very tolerable stretcher. He carried it to the kitchen where Kirsty was still sitting quite still looking into the fire.

"Kirsty," he said, "ye're almost as strong as a man, and I wouldna willingly hae any but oor own three sel's layin' a finger on what's left o' Steenie. Are ye up to helpin' me fetch him home?"

Kirsty rose at once.

"A drappy o' milk and I'm ready," she answered. "Will ye

no take a mouthful o' whiskey yersel' to keep ye warm, Father?"

"Na, na, I need naethin'," replied David.

He took the stretcher and they set out, saying nothing to the mother. She was still in her own room, and they hoped she might fall asleep.

"It reminds me o' the women gaein' to the sepulchre," said David. "Eh, but it must hae been a sore time for them!—a heap worse than this heartbreak here."

"They didna ken that he wasna dead," agreed Kirsty, "and we do ken that Steenie's no dead. He's maybe walkin' aboot wi' the bonny man—or maybe jist risin' himsel' a wee bit after the uprisin'! Jist think o' his head bein' all right, and his eyes as clear as the bonny man's own! Eh, but Steenie must be in great happiness."

Thus talking as they went, they reached the earth house. They found no angels on guard, for Steenie did not have to get up again.

David wept the few tears of an old man over the son who had been of no use in the world but the best use—to love and be loved. Then, one at the head and the other at the feet, they brought the body out and laid it on the bier.

Kirsty went in again and took Steenie's shoes, tying them in her apron.

"His feet's no sich a weight noo!" she said as together they carried their burden home.

The mother met them at the door.

"Oh!" she cried, "I thought the Lord had taken ye both, and left me alone 'cause I was hardhearted to him. But noo that he's brought ye back—and Steenie, what there is o' him, poor bairn!— I'll never say another word, but jist let him do as he likes. There, Lord, I'm done! Pardon me what ye can."

They carried the forsaken thing up the stairs and laid it on Kirsty's bed, looking so like and so unlike Steenie asleep. Marion was so exhausted, both in mind and body, that her husband insisted on her postponing all further activity till the morning. But at night Kirsty unclothed the untenanted, and put on it a long white nightgown.

When the mother saw it lying thus, she smiled, and wept no more, She knew that the bonny man had taken home his angelic idiot.

27 / From Snow to Fire

A long way from the region of heather and snow, in India in the year of the mutiny, the regiment in which Francis Gordon served, his father's old regiment, had lain for months besieged in a well-known city by the native troops, and had begun to know what privation meant. Danger and sickness, wounds and fatigue, hunger and death, had brought out the best that was in the worst of them. Francis Gordon had done his part, and well.

It would be difficult to analyze the effect of the punishment Kirsty had given him, but its influence was upon him through the whole of the terrible time. I dare hardly speculate what he might have done had she not defended herself so that he could not reach her. It is possible that Kirsty herself saved him from what would have been a horrible shame—taking revenge on a woman avenging a woman's wrong. From having deserved to be struck by a woman, nothing but repentant shame could save him.

When he came to himself, the first bitterness of the thing past, he could not avoid the conviction that his childhood playmate, whom once he loved best in the world, and who as a girl refused to marry him, had come to despise him, and righteously. The idea took a firm hold on him, and became his most frequently recurring thought. The wale of Kirsty's whip served to recall it a good many nights, especially during night watches when the time was slow, or when he had done anything his conscience called wrong, or when his judgment had been foolish.

He had not grown particularly better in India, but had kept from getting worse, and for a time at least, the poor little thing his conscience was had been rising. Events had been in his favor. After reaching India he had no time to be idle. The mutiny broke out, he had to stir himself into action, and, as I have said, the best in him was called to the front.

He was especially capable of action with show in it. Let the eyes be bent upon him and he would go far. Left to act for himself, undirected and unseen, his courage would not have proved of the highest order. Throughout the siege, when others did see him, he was noted for a daring that often left the bounds of prudence far behind. More than once he was wounded—and seriously. But even then he was back at his post in four days. His genial manners, friendly carriage, and gay endurance made him a favorite with all.

The sufferings of the besieged at length grew to the point that there was little likelihood of the approaching army being able to relieve the place. Thus orders were given by the commander in chief to abandon it: every British person must be out of the city before the night of the following day. The general in charge thereupon resolved to take advantage of the very bad watch kept by the enemy, and steal away in silence that same night.

The order was given to the companies, to each man individually, to prepare for the perilous evacuation, but to keep it absolutely secret except from those who were to accompany them. And so cautious was the little English colony as well as the garrison that not a rumor of the retreat reached the besiegers, while throughout the lines it was thoroughly understood that, at a certain hour of the night, without call of bugle or beat of drum, everyone should be prepared to leave. Ten minutes after that, the garrison was in silent motion.

The first shot of the enemy's morning salutation went tearing through a bungalow within whose shattered walls lay Francis Gordon, still slumbering wearily. He jumped up to find blood flowing from a splinter wound on his temple and cheekbone. A second shot struck the foot of the chair in which he had been lying. He sprang forward, grabbing his coat as he went.

But why was everything so still inside? No guns answered. Firing at such an early hour, the rebels must have got wind of their intended evacuation. It was too late for that, but why did not the garrison reply? Between the shots he seemed to *hear* the universal silence.

Heavens! It was daylight. He had overslept! He ought to have been with his men—how long ago he could not tell, for the first shot had taken his watch. A third came and broke his sword where it hung on the wall. Not a sound, not a murmur reached him from the fortifications.

Was the garrison gone? Was the hour past? Had no one missed him? Had no one called him?

He rushed into the compound. Not a creature was there! He was alone!—one English officer amid a revolting army of hating Indians.

But they did not yet know that their prey had slid from their grasp, for they were going on with their usual gun-reveille. He might yet elude them and overtake the garrison!

Half-dazed he hurried for the gate by which they were to leave the city.

He met no live thing on his way except for two starved dogs. One of them ran from him. The other would have followed him, but a cannonball struck the ground between them, raising a cloud of dust, and he saw no more of the dog.

He found the gate open and not one of the enemy in sight. Tokens of the retreat were plentiful, making the track he had to follow plain enough.

But now an enemy he had never encountered before all at once assailed him—a sense of loneliness and desertion and helplessness, rising to utter desolation. He had never in his life enjoyed being alone—not that he loved his neighbor, but he loved his neighbor's company, making him less aware of an uneasy self. And now he first realized that he had seen his sword hilt go off with a shot, and had not caught up his revolver—that he was, in fact, absolutely unarmed.

He quickened his pace to overtake his comrades. On and on he trudged through nothing but rice fields, the day growing hotter and hotter, and his sense of desolation increasing. Two or three natives passed him, who looked at him, he thought, with sinister eyes. He had eaten no breakfast, and was not likely to have any lunch. He grew sick and faint, but there was no refuge. He must walk, walk until he fell and could walk no more! With the heat and his exertion, his wound began to assert itself, and by and by he felt so sick that he turned off the road and lay down. While he lay, the eyes of his mind began to open to the fact that the courage he had before been so eager to show could hardly have been of the right sort . . . seeing it was now gone—thoroughly evaporated.

He rose and resumed his walk, but at every smallest sound he started in fear of a lurking foe. With regret he remembered the long-bladed dagger knife he had carried in his pocket when a boy. It was exhaustion and illness, true, that destroyed his courage, but not the less was he a man of fear, and not the less did he feel himself a coward. Again he got off the road and lay down, but in a minute or two got up again and went on, his fear growing until, mainly through consciousness of itself, it ripened into abject terror. Loneliness seemed to have taken the shape of a watching omnipresent enemy, out of whose diffusion death might at any moment break in some hideous form.

It was getting toward night when at length he saw dust ahead of him. Soon after, he thought he could make out the straggling rear of the retreating English.

Before he reached it a portion had halted for a little rest, and he was glad to lie down in a rough cart. Long before the morning the cart was on its way again, and Gordon in it, raving with fever, was unable to tell who he was. He was soon in a friendly shelter, however, under skillful medical treatment, and was nursed tenderly.

When at length he seemed to have almost recovered his health, it was clear that he had in great measure lost his reason.

Things were going from bad to worse at Castle Weelset.

Whether Mrs. Gordon had disgusted her friends or got tired of them, I do not know, but she remained at home, seldom had a visitor, and never a guest. Rumor, busy in country as in town, said she was more and more manifesting herself a slave to strong drink. She was so tired of herself that, to escape her double, she made it increasingly a bore to her. She never read a book, never had a newspaper sent her, never inquired how things were going on about the place or in any part of the world, did nothing for herself or others, only ate, drank, slept, and raged at those around her.

One morning David Barclay, having occasion to see the factor, went to the castle. He found him at home ill. So David thought he would make an attempt to see Mrs. Gordon and offer what service he could. She might not have forgotten that in old days he had been a good deal about the estate.

She received him at once, but behaved in such extraordinary fashion that he could not have any doubt she was at least half drunk. There was no sense, David said, either to be got out of her or put into her.

At Corbyknowe they heard nothing of the young laird. The papers said a good deal about the state of things in India, but Francis Gordon was not mentioned.

In the autumn of the year 1858, when the days were growing short, and the nights cold in the high region about the Horn, the son of a neighboring farmer, who had long desired to know Kirsty better, called at Corbyknowe with his sister, ostensibly on business with David. They were shown into the parlor, and all were sitting together in the early gloaming, the young woman bent on persuading Kirsty to pay them a visit and see the improvements they had made in house and garden, and the two farmers lamenting the affairs of the property on which they were tenants, and which was going so rapidly downhill under the total absence of management of Mrs. Gordon.

"But I hear there's a new grief likely to come to the auld lairdship," said William Lammie as he sat with an elbow on the tea table from which Kirsty was removing the crumbs.

"And what wisdom o' the countryside may they be puttin' forth noo?" asked David, in a tone of good-humored irony.

"Weel, I hear Mistress Comrie's been to Edinbro' for a week or two, and's come home wi' a gey odd story concernin' the yoong laird—away oot there whaur there's been sich a rumpus wi' the heathen soldiers. There's word come, she says, that he's fallen into the very glare o' disgrace, shirkin' back frae somethin' they gave him to do: na, he jist wouldna do it! And they had him afore a court-martial, as they call it, and showed him to be jist a bare cooward. He'll hae an ill time o' it, showin' the face o' him again in his own country!"

"It's a lie," said Kirsty. "I'll take my oath upon it, whoever telled it. There never was a mark o' cooward upon Francie Gordon. He had his faults, but no one o' them looked that way. He was kind o' weak sometimes, and unco easy come over, but, haein' little fear mysel', I ken a cooward when I see him. Something may hae set up his pride—he has enough o' that for two devils—but Francie was never nae cooward!"

"Dinna lay the lie at my door, I beg ye, Miss Barclay. I was but tellin' ye what fowk was sayin'."

"Fowk's aye sayin', and seldom sayin' true. The worst o' it is that honest fowk's aye ready to believe lies! They dinna lie themsel's and sae it's no easy to them to think another would. They're no all liars that spreads the lie; but for them that makes the lie, the Lord silence them!"

"Hoots, Kirsty!" said her mother, "it doesna become ye to curse naebody! It's no right o' ye!"

"It's a good Bible curse, Mother. It's naethin' but a way o' sayin' 'his will be done.' "

"Ye needna be sae strong in yer defense o' the laird, Miss Barclay! He was nae particular friend o' yours if all the tales be true!" remarked her admirer.

"I'm tellin' ye tales is mostly lies. I hae kenned the laird since he was a wee laddie—and afore that. And I'm nae gaein' to hear him lied aboot and hold my tongue. A lie's a lie, whether the liar be a liar or not. There! I hae done wi' it!"

She did not speak another word to him except to bid him good night.

In the beginning of the year, a rumor went about the country that the laird had been seen at the castle, but it died away.

David pondered, but asked no questions, and Mrs. Bremner volunteered no information.

Kirsty of course heard the rumor, but she never took much interest in the goings on at the castle. Mrs. Gordon's doings were not such as the angels desire to look into. And Kirsty, related to them in not such a distant way, inherited a good many of their heavenly peculiarities, and minded her own business.

29 / One January Night

One night in the month of January, when the snow was falling thick, but the air, because of the cloud blankets overhead, was not piercing, Kirsty went out to the workshop to tell her father that supper was ready. David was a jack-of-all-trades—therein resembling a sailor rather than a soldier, and by the light of a single dip candle was busy with some bit of carpenter's work.

He did not raise his head when she entered, and heard her as if he did not hear. She wondered a little and waited. After a few moments of silence, he said quietly, without looking up—

"Are ye aware o' anythin' oot o' the ordinary, Kirsty?"

"Na, naethin', father," she answered, still wondering.

"It's been bearin' itsel' in upon me at my bench here, that Steenie's aboot the place tonight. I canna help imaginin' he's been upon this very floor over and over again since I came oot, as if he would tell me somethin', but couldna, and gaed away again."

"Do ye think he's here this moment, Father?"

"No, not now."

"He used to sometimes think the bonny man was aboot," said Kirsty reflectively.

"My mither was a highlan' wuman, and had the second sight. There was nae doobt aboot it," remarked David, also thoughtfully.

"And what would ye draw frae that, Father?" asked Kirsty.

"Ow, naethin' very important, maybe, but jist possibly that it might be in the family."

Kirsty was silent a moment, then turned her face toward the farthest corner. The place was rather large and everywhere dark except within the narrow circle of the candlelight. In a quiet voice, with a little quaver in it, she said aloud, "If ye be here, Steenie, an' the bonny man be wi' ye, and ye hae the power, let us ken if there be anythin' lyin' to oor hand that ye wish done. I'm sure if there be, it's for oor sakes and no for ye ain, glad as we would be to do anythin' for ye; the bonny man lets ye want for naethin, we're sure o' that."

"Ay we are, Steenie," assented his father.

No voice came from the darkness. They stood silent for a while. Then David said, "Go in, lassie. Yer mither'll be wonderin' what's come o' ye. I'll be there in a minute. I hae jist the last stroke to give this bit o' jobby."

Without a word, but with disappointment in her heart that Steenie had not answered them, Kirsty obeyed. But she went round through the rickyard so that she might have a moment's thought with herself.

Not a hand was laid upon her out of the darkness, no faintest sound came to her ears through the silently falling snow. But as she took her way between two ricks, where there was just room for her to pass, she felt—felt, however, without the slightest sense of *material* opposition, that she could not go through.

Trying afterward to describe what rather she was aware of than felt, she said the nearest she could come to it, but it was not right either, was to say that she seemed to encounter the ghost of solidity. Certainly nothing seemed to touch her. She made no attempt to overcome the resistance, and the moment she turned, knew herself free to move in any other direction. But as the house was still her goal, she tried another space between two of the ricks. There again she found she could not pass. Making a third essay in yet another space, she was once more stopped in like fashion.

With that came the conviction that she was wanted elsewhere, and with it the thought of the Horn. She turned her face from the house and made straight for the hill, only that she took, as she had generally done with Steenie, the easier and rather longer way.

The notion of the presence of the bonny man, with perhaps Steenie at his side, which had been with her all the time, naturally suggested Steenie's house as the spot where she was wanted, and she sped quickly there. But the moment she reached it, almost before she entered, she felt as if it were utterly empty—as if it had not in it even enough air to give her breath.

When a place seems to repel us, when we feel as if we could not live there, what if the cause be that there are no souls in it making it comfortable to the spiritual sense? That the knowledge of such presence would make most people uneasy is no argument against the fancy. Truth itself, its intrinsic, essential, necessary trueness unrecognized, must be repellent.

Kirsty did not remain a moment in Steenie's house, but set her face to go home by the shorter and rougher path leading over the earth house and across the little burn.

The night continued dark, with an occasional thinning of the obscurity when some high current blew the clouds aside from a little nest of stars. Just as Kirsty reached the descent to the burn, the snow ceased, the clouds parted, and a faint worn moon appeared. It looked just like a little old lady too thin and too tired to go on living more than a night longer. But her waning life was yet potent over Kirsty; and her strange, wasted beauty, dying to rise again, made Kirsty glad as she went down the hill through the snow-crowned heather. The oppression that came on her in Steenie's house was entirely gone; and in the face of the pale, ancient moon, her heart grew so light that she broke into a silly song which, while they were still children, she had made for Steenie, who had never tired of listening to it:

> Willy, wally, woo!
> Hame comes the coo—
> Hummle, bummle, moo!—
> Widin ower to Bogie,
> Hame to fill the cogie!

Bonny hummle coo,
Wi' her baggy fu
O' butter and o' milk,
And cream as saft as silk,
A' gethered frae the gerse
Intil her tassly purse,
To be oors, no hers,
Gudewillie, hummle coo!
Willy, wally, woo!
Moo, Hummlie, moo!

Singing this childish rhyme, dear to the slow-waking soul of Steenie, she had come almost to the bottom of the hill and was just stepping over the top of her earth house when something like a groan startled her.

She stopped and sent a keen-searching glance around. It came again, muffled and dull. It must be from the earth house.

Somebody was there! It could not be Steenie, for why should Steenie groan? But he might be calling for her, and the house changed the character of the sound! Anyhow, she must be wanted, so in she dived.

She could scarcely light the candle for the trembling of her hand and the beating of her heart. Slowly the flame grew, and the glimmer began to spread.

She stood speechless and stared.

Out of the darkness at her feet grew the form, as it seemed, of Steenie, lying on his face, just as when she found him there a year before. She dropped on her knees beside him.

He was alive at least, for he moved!

His face was turned away from her, and his arm was under it. The arm next to her lay out on the stones, and she took the ice-cold hand in hers: it was not Steenie's!

She took the candle and leaned across to see the face. God in heaven! there was the mark of the whip: it was Francie Gordon!

She tried to rouse him. She could not; he was cold as ice and seemed all but dead. But for the groan she had heard she would have been sure he was dead.

She blew out the light, and swift as her hands could move, took garment after garment off her and laid them all, warm from her own live heart, over and under him—all but one which she thought too thin to do him any good. Last of all she drew her stockings over his hands and arms, and, leaving her shoes where Steenie's had lain, darted out of the cave.

At the mouth of it she rose erect like one escaped from the tomb, and sped in dim-gleaming whiteness over the snow, scarce to be seen against it. The moon was but a shred—a withered autumn leaf low fallen toward the dim plain of the west. As she ran she would have seemed to one of Steenie's angels, out that night on the hill, as a newly disembodied ghost fleeing home. Swift and shadowless as the thought of her own brave heart, she ran. Her sense of power and speed was glorious. She felt—not thought—herself a human goddess, the daughter of the Eternal.

Up height and down hollow she flew, running her race with death, not an open eye, other than the eyes of her father and mother, within miles of her in a world of sleep and snow and night. She did not slacken her pace as she drew near the house; she only ran more softly. At last she threw the door to the wall and shot up the steep stairs to her room, calling her mother as she went.

30 / Back From the Grave

When David came in to supper, he said nothing, expecting Kirsty every moment to appear. Marion was the first to ask what had become of her. David answered that she had left him in the workshop.

"Bless the bairn, what can she be aboot this time o' night?" said her mother.

"I kenna," returned David.

When they had sat eating their supper for ten minutes, expecting Kirsty in vain, David went out to look for her. Returning unsuccessful, he found that Marion had been all over the house seeking her with like result. Then they first became uneasy.

Before going to look for Kirsty, however, David had begun to suspect her absence in one way or another connected with the subject of their conversation in the workshop, to which he had not alluded to his wife. When he now told her what had passed, he was a little surprised to find that immediately she grew calm.

"Ow, then, she'll be wi' Steenie," she said.

And her patience did not fail after that, but revived that of her husband. They could not, however, go to bed, but sat by the fire, saying a word or two now and then. The slow minutes passed, and neither of them moved, except David once to put on more peat.

The house door flew suddenly open and they heard Kirsty cry, "Mother, Mother!" But when they hastened to the door, no one was there. However, they heard the door of her room close, and Marion went up the stairs.

By the time she reached her, Kirsty was in a thick dress and buttoned up cloth jacket, had a pair of shoes on her bare feet, and was a glowing rosy red. David stood where he was, and in half a minute Kirsty came in three leaps down the stairs to him to say that Francie was lying in the Pict house.

In less than a minute the old soldier was out with the stable lantern harnessing one of the horses, the oldest in the stable, good at standing, and not a bad walker. He called for no help, yet was round at the door so speedily as to astonish even Kirsty, who stood with her mother in the entrance by a pile of bedding. They put a mattress in the bottom of the cart, and plenty of blankets. Kirsty got in, lay down and covered herself to make the rough ambulance warm, and David drove off. They soon reached the house and entered it.

The moment Kirsty had lighted the candle, her father exclaimed, "Lassie, there's been a wuman here!"

"It looks like it," answered Kirsty. "I was here mysel'!"

"Ay, ay, o' coorse, but there's wuman's clothes. Whaur came they frae?"

"They're mine, Father," she explained as she stooped to remove from Francis' face the garment that covered his head.

"The Lord preserve us!—to the very stockings on his hands?"

"I had no fear, Father, o' the Lord seein' me as he made me."

"Lassie," cried David with heartfelt admiration, "ye should hae been daughter to a field marshall!"

"I wouldna be daughter to a king!" returned Kirsty. "If I could be born again, I wouldna be born to any except it be David Barclay."

"My ain lassie!" murmured her father. "But, eh," he added, interrupting his own thoughts, "We must hold oor tongues till we've done the thing we're sent to do!"

They bent at once to their task.

David was a strong man still, and Kirsty was as good at a lift as most men. They had no difficulty in raising Gordon between them, David taking his head and Kirsty his feet, but it was not without difficulty they got him through the earthen passage. In the cart they covered him so that had he been a new-born baby, he could have taken no harm except it were by suffocation; and then, Kirsty sitting with his head in her lap, they drove home as fast as the old horse could step out.

In the meantime, Marion had got her best room ready and warm. When they reached it, Francis was certainly still alive, and they made haste to lay him in the hot featherbed. In about an hour they thought he swallowed a little milk. Neither Kirsty nor her parents went to bed that night, and by one or other of them the patient was constantly attended.

Kirsty took the first watch, and was satisfied that his breathing gradually grew more regular, and by and by stronger. After a while it became like that of one in a troubled sleep. He moved his head a little and murmured like one dreaming painfully. She called her father and told him Francis was saying words she could not understand. He took her place and sat near him, when presently, his soldier-ears still sharp, David heard indications of a hot siege. Once Francis started up on his elbow, and put his hand to the side of his head. For a moment he looked wildly awake, then sank back and went to sleep again.

As Marion was by him in the morning, all at once he spoke again, and more plainly.

"Go away, Mother!" he said. "I am not mad. I am only troubled in my mind. I will tell my father you killed me."

Marion tried to rouse him, telling him his mother should not come near him. He did not seem to understand, but apparently her words soothed him, for he went to sleep once more.

He was gaunt and ghastly to look at. The scar on his face, which Kirsty had taken for the mark of her whip, but which was left by the splinter that woke him, remained red and disfiguring. But the worst of his look was in his eyes, whose glances wandered about uneasy and searching. It was clear all was not right within his brain. I doubt if any other of his tenants would have recognized him.

For a good many days he was like one awake, yet dreaming, always dreading something, invariably starting when the door opened, and when quietest would lie gazing at the one by his bedside as if puzzled. He took in general what food they brought him, but at times altogether refused it. They never left him alone for more than a moment.

So far were they from turning him over to his mother that the very idea of letting her know he was with them never entered the mind of one of them. To the doctor, whom at once they had called in, there was no need to explain the right by which they constituted themselves his guardians. Anyone would have judged it better for him to be with them than with her. David said to himself that when Francie wanted to leave them, he should go. But he had sought refuge with them and he should have it. Nothing would make David give him up except legal compulsion.

31 / Francis' Awakening

One morning Francis started to his elbow as if to get up. Seeing Kirsty sitting beside him, he lay back down with his eyes fixed upon her. She glanced at him now and then, but would not seem to notice him. He gazed for two or three minutes and then said, in a low, doubtful, almost timid voice, "Kirsty?"

"Ay, what is it, Francie?" she returned.

"Is it really yersel'?" he said.

"Ay, who else, Francie?"

"Are ye angry at me, Kirsty?"

"Not a grain. What makes ye ask such a question?"

"Eh, but ye gave me such a one wi' yer whip—jist here on the temple! Look!"

He turned the side of his head toward her and stroked the place, like a small, self-pitying child. Kirsty went to him and kissed it like a mother. She had plainly perceived that such a scar could not be from her blow, but it added grievously to her pain at the remembrance of it that the poor head which she had struck had in the very same place been torn by a splinter—for so the doctor said. If her whip left any mark, the splinter had obliterated it.

"And then," he resumed, "ye called me a cooward."

"Did I do that, ill woman that I was!" she returned, with tenderest maternal soothing.

He laid his arms round her neck, drew her feebly toward him, and wept.

Kirsty put her arm round him, held him closer, and stroked

his head with her other hand, murmuring words of much meaning though little sense. He drew back his head, looked at her beseechingly, and said,

"*Do* ye think me a cooward, Kirsty?"

"No wi' men," answered the truthful girl, who would not lie even in ministration to a mind diseased.

"Maybe ye think I ought to hae struck ye back when ye struck me? I *will* be a cooward then, let ye say what ye like. I never did, and I never will, hit a lassie, let her kill me!"

"It wasna that, Francie. If I called ye a cooward, it was 'cause ye behaved ill to Phemy.

"Oh, the bonny little Phemy! I had almost forgotten her. Hoo is she, Kirsty?"

"She's weel—and very weel," answered Kirsty. "She's dead."

"Dead!" echoed Gordon with a cry, again raising himself on his elbow. "Surely it wasna—it wasna that the poor wee thing couldna forget me! The thing's no possible! I wasna worth it!"

"Na, na, it wasna that. Her dyin' had naethin' to do wi' that—or wi' you in any way. I dinna believe she was a hair worse for any o' the nonsense ye said to her. She died on the Horn in an awful storm. She couldna hae suffered long, poor thing. She hadna the strength to suffer muckle. Sae away she gaed!—and Steenie after her," added Kirsty in a lower tone, but Francis did not seem to hear, and said no more for a while.

"But I must tell ye the truth, Kirsty," he resumed. "Besides yersel', there's them that says I'm a cooward."

"I heard a man say that, only one. And him only once."

"And ye said to him, 'Ay. I hae long kenned that!' "

"I told him whoever said it was a liar!"

"But ye believe it yersel', Kirsty!"

"Would ye hae me liar and hypocrite besides, to call fowk ill names for sayin' what I believe mysel'!"

"But I *am* a cooward, Kirsty!"

"Ye are *not*, Francie. I wunna believe it though ye say it

yersel'. It's naethin' but a speck o' the dust o' nonsense that's got through the cracks ye got in yer head frae fightin'. Ye was aye a daft kind o' creature, Francie! If onybody ever said it, make speed and get yer health back again, and then ye can show him plain that he's a liar."

"But I tell ye, Kirsty, I ran away!"

"I fancy ye would hae been naethin' but a muckle idiot if ye hadna! Ye didna leave onybody in trouble, did ye?"

"Not a soul I ken o'. Na, I didna do that. The fact was—but nae blame to them—they all gaed away and left me alone sleepin'. I must hae been terrible tired!"

"I telled ye sae!" cried Kirsty. "Jist go over the story to me, Francie, and I'll tell ye whether ye're a cooward or no. I dinna believe an atom o' it. Ye never was, and is never likely to be a cooward."

But Francis showed such signs of excitement as well as exhaustion that Kirsty saw she must not let him talk longer.

"Or I'll tell ye what," she added; "—ye can tell Father and Mother and me the whole tale tonight, or maybe tomorrow mornin'. Ye must hae an egg noo, and a drappy o' milk—creamy milk, Francie. Ye aye liked that."

She went and prepared the little meal, and after taking it he went to sleep.

In the evening, with the help of their questioning, he told them everything he could recall from the moment he woke to find the place abandoned, not omitting his terrors on the way, until he overtook the rear of the garrison.

"I dinna wonder ye were frightened, Francie," said Kirsty. "I would hae been afraid mysel' wi'oot a sword and kennin' nae God to trust in. Ye must learn to ken him, Francie, and then ye'll be feared at naethin'!"

After that, his memory was only of utterly confused shapes, many of which must have been fancies. The only things he could report were the conviction pervading them all that he had disgraced himself, and the consciousness that everyone treated him as a deserter and gave him the cold shoulder.

His next recollection was of coming home to, or rather finding himself with his mother, who, the moment she saw him, flew into a rage, struck him in the face, and called him a coward. She must have taken him, he thought, to some place where there were people about who would not let him alone, but he could remember nothing more until he found himself creeping into a hole that he seemed to know, thinking he was a fox with hounds after him.

"What's my clothes like, Kirsty?" he asked at this point.

"They were no that grand," answered Kirsty, her eyes smarting with the coming tears. "But ye'll never see a stitch o' them again: I put them away."

"Hoo will I get up wi'oot them?" he rejoined, with a tremor of anxiety in his voice.

"We'll see aboot that; there's time enough," answered Kirsty.

"But my mither may be after me. I would fain be up! There's no sayin' what she mightna be up to. She canna bide me."

"Dread ye naethin', Francie. Ye're maybe no match for her, but I'll be atween the two o' ye. She's no sae fearsome as she thinks. Anyway, she doesna frighten me!"

"I left some good clothes there when I gaed away, and I daresay they're in my room yet—if I only kenned hoo to get at them!"

"I'll go and get them to ye—the very day ye're fit to rise. But ye mustn't speak a word more tonight."

32 / Kirsty Stirs Herself to Action

They held a long consultation that night as to what they must do.

One of the first and most important things was to rid Francis of the delusion that he had disgraced himself in the eyes of his fellow officers. He must be made to feel like a man again. This would wake him from the bad dream to the reality of his condition, and then he could resume his place in the march of his generation through life.

To find a way to accomplish this, they set their wits to work. It became clear at once that the readiest way would be to attempt to communicate with any they could reach of the officers under whom he had served. However, by this time his regiment, along with the rest of the Company's soldiers, had passed into the service of the Queen from the East India Company, a change on which Francis would undoubtedly give no further information. David decided to apply to Sir Haco Macintosh, who had succeeded Archibald Gordon in the command for assistance in finding who might have the information he wanted.

"Don't ye think, Father," said Kirsty, "that it would be the surest and speediest way for me to go mysel' to Sir Haco?"

" 'Deed it would be that, Kirsty," answered David. "The bodily presence is always stronger than a letter."

Although at first she was a little appalled at the thought of Kirsty alone in such a huge city as Edinburgh, Marion could not help assenting to the wisdom of her husband. Therefore the next morning Kirsty started, bearing a letter from her father to his old officer.

Sir Haco had retired from the service some years before the mutiny and was living in one of the serenely gloomy squares in the Scots capital. Kirsty left her letter at the door, and then called the next day. She was shown into the library, where lady Macintosh as well as Sir Haco awaited her, with curious and kindly interest in the daughter of the man they had known so well and respected so much.

When Kirsty entered the room, dressed very simply in a gown of dark cloth and a plain straw bonnet, the impression she at once made was more than favorable, and they received her with a kindness and courtesy that made her feel welcome. They were indeed of her own kind.

Sir Haco was one of the few men who, regarding constantly the reality, not the show of things, keep throughout their life, however long, a great part of their youth and all their childhood. Deeper far in his heart than any of the honors he had received, all unsought but none undeserved, lay the memory of a happy and reverential boyhood. Sprung from a peasant stock, his father was a simple, courteous, and respectful man whom the young Haco greatly loved.

He was well matched with his wife, who, though born to a far higher social position in which simplicity is rarer, was, like him, true and humble and strong. They had one daughter, who grew up only to die. The moment they saw Kirsty, their hearts went out to her.

For there was in Kirsty that unassumed, unconscious dignity, that simple propriety, that naturalness of carriage, neither restrained nor warped by thought of self, which at once wakes confidence and regard; while her sweet, unaffected "book English," with no disastrous endeavor to avoid her own country's accent, revealed at once her genuine cultivation.

Listening to her first words, and reminded of the solemn sententious way in which Sergeant Barclay used to express himself, his face rose clear in Haco's mind's eye, he saw it as it were reflected in his daughter's, and broke out with, "Oh, lassie, but ye're like yer father!"

"Ye remember him, sir?" rejoined Kirsty.

"Remember him! Naebody worth his rememberin' could forget him! Sit ye doon, and tell us all aboot him!"

Kirsty did as she was told. She began at the beginning and explained the relation between her father and Colonel Gordon, and how he had always felt it his business to look after the young laird. Then she told him of the return of Francis and the unanswered questions that had been raised, hoping, she said, that Sir Haco might be able to direct her toward someone who could provide them with the sort of information they sought.

"And what sort of information do you think I can give or get for you, Miss Barclay?" asked Sir Haco.

Thereupon Kirsty told the story in more detail of Francis' escape, his fears, and, with some elucidatory suggestions of her own, his obsession with thinking himself a coward.

When their interview was at an end, Sir Haco and Lady Macintosh insisted on Kirsty's remaining with them while she was in Edinburgh; and Kirsty, partly in the hope of expediting the object of her mission thereby, and partly because her heart was drawn to her new friends, gladly consented. Before a week was over, her hostess felt as if Kirsty were a daughter until now long waiting for her somewhere in the infinite.

That very same morning, Sir Haco sat down to his study table and began writing to every officer he could recall who had served with Francis Gordon, requesting to know his feelings and that of the regiment about him. Within three days he received the first of the answers, which kept dropping in for the next six months. They all described Gordon as rather a scatterbrain, as not the less a favorite with officers and men, and as always showing the courage of a man, or rather of a boy, seeing he not infrequently acted with a reprehensible recklessness that smacked a little of showing off.

"That's Francie!" cried Kirsty, when her host read the first such, which had come as the result of his inquiry.

Within two weeks he also received, from one high in office, the assurance that if Mr. Gordon, on his recovery, wished to enter

Her Majesty's service, he should have his commission.

While her husband was thus occupied, Lady Macintosh was showing Kirsty every loving attention she could think of, and took her about Edinburgh and its neighborhood, finding in the process that the country girl knew far more of the history of Scotland than she did herself.

As soon as Kirsty felt she could do so without seeming ungrateful for their extreme hospitality, she bade her new friends farewell, and hurried home with copies of the answers which Sir Haco had till that time received.

When she arrived, her heart was so glad that she laughed merrily at the sight of Francis in her father's Sunday clothes. Haggard as he looked, the old twinkle awoke in his eye from her joyous amusement. David came in the next moment from putting up the gray mare with which he had met the coach to bring Kirsty home, and saw the two of them along with Marion laughing in such an abandonment of mirth that he could not help joining in, though completely unaware of the immediate motive.

The same evening Kirsty went to the castle. Mrs. Bremner needed no persuasion to find the suit that the young laird had left in his room. She willingly gave it to Kirsty to take to its owner. When he woke the next morning, Francis saw the gray garment lying by his bedside in place of David's black one, and felt immediately better for it.

The letters Kirsty had brought, working along with returning health, and the surrounding love and sympathy most potent of all, speedily dispelled his yet lingering delusion. It had occasionally returned very strongly while Kirsty was away, but now it left him altogether.

33 / A Great Gulf and a Great Rising⸻

It was now midsummer, and Francis Gordon was well, though looking thin and rather delicate. Kirsty and he had walked together to the top of the Horn, and there sat in the heart of old memories. The sun was clouded above. The boggy basin lay dark below, with its rim of heathery hills not yet in bloom, and its bottom of peaty marsh, green and black, with here and there a shining spot. The growing crops of the far-off farms on the other side but little affected the general impression the view gave of a waste world. Yet the wide expanse of heaven and earth lifted Kirsty's heart with an indescribable sense of presence, purpose, and promise. For was it not the country on which, fresh from God, she first opened the eyes of this life, the visible region in which all her efforts had gone forth, in which all the food of her growth had been gathered, in which all her joys had come to her, in which all her loves had their scope, the place whence by and by she would go away to find her brother with the bonny man!

Francis looked without heeding, saw without seeing. His heart was not uplifted. His earthly future, a future of his own imagining, drew him, just as it had that day so long ago when the two had been talking and had ended with a foot race along the flank of the Horn.

"This won't do any longer, Kirsty!" he said at length. "The accusing angel'll be upon me again before I know it. I mustn't be idle 'cause I'm happy once more—thanks to you, Kirsty! I never thought I'd be able to raise my head again. But now I must get back to my work. I'm fit enough!"

"I'm right glad to hear it," answered Kirsty. "I was jist thinkin' o' somethin' o' the same sort, but I didna want to be the first to say it."

"Why not, Kirsty?"

" 'Cause I wouldna hae ye do something jist to please me."

"Why?"

" 'Cause it would show ye're no a man yet! A man's a man that does what's right, what's pleasin' to the very heart o' right. Ye'll please me best by no tryin' to please me. And ye'll please God best by doin' what he's puttin' into yer heart as the right thing, and the bonny thing, and the true thing. Tell me what ye're thinkin' o' doin'."

"What but going after this new commission they have promised me. There's a good chance of fighting on the borders—the frontiers, as they call them."

Kirsty sat silent. She had been thinking a great deal about what Francis ought to do, and had changed her mind about it since the time she and Sir Haco talked about his entering the Queen's service.

"Isn't that what you would have me do, Kirsty?" he said, when he found she continued silent. "A body's not a fool for wanting good advice."

"Na, that's true enough! What for would ye want to go fightin'?"

"To show the world I'm none of what my mother called me."

"And showin' that, hoo muckle the better man would ye be for it? Mind ye, it's one thing to be and another to show. *Be* ye must; *show* ye needna."

"I don't know. I might be growing better all the time."

"And ye might be growin' worse. What the better would any neighbor be for gaein' fightin'? Wouldna it all be for yersel'? Is there naethin' given into yer hand to do—naethin' nearer home than that? Surely o' two things, one near and one far, the near comes first!"

"I thought ye wanted me to go."

"Ay, rather than bide at home doin' naethin'. But mightna there be somethin' better to do?"

"I don't know. I thought the commission would please you, but it seems nothing will."

"Ay, that's whaur the mischief lies: ye thought to please *me*!"

"I did think to please you, Kirsty! I thought once I had done well afore the world, as my father did, I might have the face to come home to you, and say, 'Kirsty, will ye hae me noo?' "

"Aye the same auld Francie!" sighed Kirsty, with a deep sigh.

"Well?"

"I tell ye, Francie, I'll never hae ye on any sich terms! Suppose I was to marry somebody when ye was away provin' yersel' and all the rest that never doobted ye, that ye was a brave man—what would ye do when ye came home?"

"Nothing of mortal good! Take to the drink maybe."

"Ye tell me that, and then ye think, wi' my eyes open, that I would marry ye?—a man like that? Eh, Francie, Francie! Ye make my heart sore, Francie. I hae done my best wi' ye, and this is the end o' it!"

"For the life of me, Kirsty, I don't know what you're driving at, or what you would have me do!"

"Man, did ye never once in yer life think what ye ought to do—what ye *had* to do—what was given ye to do—what it was yer duty to do? Do ye think only o' appearances and never o' what's the right and honorable thing?"

"Not so often, I'm sure, as I should. But I'm ready to hear you tell me my duty. I'm not past reasoning with!"

"Did ye never hear that ye're to love yer neighbor as yersel'?"

"I'm doing that with all my heart, Kirsty—and that you know as well as I do myself."

"You mean me, Francie! And ye call that loving me, to wish me to marry a man that's no a man yet! But it's not me that's yer neighbor, Francie!"

"Who *is* my neighbor, Kirsty?"

"The question's been asked afore—and answered."

"And what's the answer to it?"

"That yer neighbor's jist whoever lies next to ye in need o' yer help. If ye read the tale o' the good Samaritan wi' any sort o' gumption, that's what ye'll read in it, and naethin' else. The man or woman ye can help, ye hae to be neighbor to."

"I want to help you."

"Ye canna help me. I'm no in need o' yer help. And the question's no whaur's the man I *might* help, but whaur's the man I *must* help. I wanted to be yer neighbor when we were yoong, and still do, but I couldna get at ye for the thieves. Ye *would* stick to them, and they wouldna let me do naethin'."

"What thieves, in the name of common sense, Kirsty? I don't know what you're talking about!"

"Love o' yer own way, and love o' makin' a show, and no care o' doin' what's right jist for truth's sake. Ah, Francie, I dinna doobt something a heap worse'll hae to come upon ye to help ye see—really *see*—the way God's world is. My labor's lost on ye, and I dearly grudge it—no the labor, but the loss o' it. I grudge that sore!"

"Kirsty, in the name of God, who *is* my neighbor?"

"Yer ain mither."

"My mother!—*her* out of the whole world? I never came upon so much as a spark of reason in her!"

"Mightna she be that one oot o' all the world that ye never showed a spark o' reason to?"

"There's no place in her for reason to get in!"

"Ye never tried her wi' it. Ye would argue wi' her plenty, but did ye ever show her reason in yer behavior?"

"Well, you *are* turning against me—you that's saved my life from her! Didn't I tell you how, when I made it home at last and went to her, for she was always good to me when I wasn't well, she fell out on me like a very devil, raging and calling me horrible names. In the end I just ran from the house—and you know where you found me. If it hadn't been for you, I would have been dead: I was worse than dead already. How *can* I be a neighbor to *her*!

It would be nothing but cat and dog between us from morning to night!''

"One body canna be cat and dog both. And the dog's as ill as the cat—sometimes worse.''

"Any dog would howl if you threw a kettle of boiling water over him!''

"She did that to ye?''

"She tried. I ran from her. She had the toddy kettle in her hand, and she splashed it in her own face trying to fling it at me.''

"Maybe she didna ken ye.''

"She knew me well enough. She called me by my own as well as other names.''

"Ye're jist addin' to my argument, Francie. Yer mither's per-ishin' o' drink! She drinks and drinks, and, by what I hear, cares for naethin' else. All's on the road to ruin in her and aboot her. She hasna the brains noo, if ever she had them, to guide hersel'. Is Satan to hold her 'cause ye winna be neighbor to her and fight him off her? I ken ye're a good son sae far as to let her do as she likes and take most o' the siller; but that's what greases the axle o' the cart the devil's gotten her into! I ken weel she hasna been muckle o' a mither to ye, but ye're her son when all's said and done. And there can be naethin' ye're called upon to do, sae long as she's in the grip o' the enemy, other than to pull her oot o' it. If ye dinna do that, ye'll never be oot o' his grip yersel'. Ye come oot together, or ye bide together.''

Gordon sat speechless.

"It's impossible!'' he said at length.

"Francie,'' rejoined Kirsty, very quietly and solemnly, "ye're yer mither's keeper. Ye're her nearest neighbor. Are ye gaein' to do yer duty by her or are ye not?''

"I canna. I darena. I'm a cooward afore her,'' he replied, reverting to the speech of his childhood.

"If ye let her go on to disgrace yer father, no to say yersel', I'll say mysel' that ye're a cooward. Bravery's no always fightin' another foe who holds a rifle or is tryin' to kill ye. It takes a deeper kind o' strength to be a man—a brave man!—in things o' the heart and soul."

"Come home wi' me, Kirsty, and take my part, and I'll promise ye to do my best."

"Ye must take yer own part, and ye must take her part too against her worse sel'."

"It's not to be thought of, Kirsty!"

"Ye winna?"

"I can't alone. I wouldn't even try it. It would be worse than useless."

Kirsty rose, turning her face homeward. Gordon sprang to his feet. She was already three yards from him.

"Kirsty, Kirsty!" he cried, going after her and laying his hand on her arm.

She stopped and faced him, but said not a word. He dropped his hand. His face was white.

"Kirsty! Won't you even speak to me?"

"I've said what there is to say, Francie. It's no for me I'm urgin' ye to open yer eyes. It's for yersel'! Ye asked me who was yer neighbor, and I told ye as best as I understood it. Lovin' the one closest by ye's the only way into the life ye're still wantin'. There's naethin' else to say till ye want that life yersel'. But I canna make ye want it, Francie."

She looked deep into his eyes, then turned and walked on again.

Like one in a dream he followed, his head hanging, his eyes on the heather. She went on faster. He gradually fell behind her but hardly knew it. Down and down the hill he followed, and only at the earth house lifted his head. She was already nearly over the opposite brae! He had let her go. He might still have overtaken her, but he knew that he had lost her.

He had no home, no refuge!

Then for the first time in his life, not even when alone in the beleaguered city, he knew desolation. He had never knocked at the door of heaven, and earth had closed hers! An angel who needed no flaming sword to make her awful held the gate of his lost paradise against him. None but she could open to him, and he knew that, like God himself, Kirsty was inexorable. Left alone with that last terrible look from the eyes of the one being he loved, he threw himself in despair on the ground. True love is an awful thing, not to the untrue only, but sometimes to the growing true, for to everything that can be burned it is a consuming fire. Never more, it seemed, would those eyes look in at his soul's window without that sad, indignant repudiation in them! He rose, and crept into the earth house.

Kirsty lost herself in prayer as she went. "Lord, I hae done all I can!" she said. "Until you hae done somethin' by yersel', I can do naethin' more. He's in yer hands still, I praise thee, though he's oot o' mine! Lord, if I hae done him any ill, forgive me. A poor human body canna ken always the best! Dinna let him suffer for my ignorance, whether I be to blame for it or no. I will try to do whatever ye make plain to me, Lord."

By the time she reached home she was calm. Her mother saw and respected her solemn mood, gave her a mother's look, and said nothing. She knew that Kirsty, lost in her own thoughts, was in good company.

What was passing in the soul of Francis Gordon, I can only indicate; I cannot show in detail. The most mysterious of all vital movements, a generation, a transition, was there—how initiated, God only knows. Francis knew neither whence it came nor whither it went. He was being reborn from above. The change was in himself; the birth was that of his will. It was his own highest action, therefore all God's. He was passing from death into life, and knew it no more than the babe knows that he is being born. The change was into a new state of being, of the very existence of which most men are incredulous, for it is beyond preconception, capable only of being experienced. Thorough as is the change, the man knows himself the same man, and yet would rather cease to be than return to what he was. The unknown germ in him, the root of his being, yea, his very being itself, the holy thing which is his intrinsic substance, hitherto unknown to his consciousness, has begun to declare itself. The caterpillar is passing into the butterfly. It is a change in which God is the potent presence, but which the man or woman must will into being or remain the jailer who prisons in loathsomeness his own God-born self, and chokes the fountain of his own liberty.

Francis knew nothing of all this. He only felt that he must knock at the door behind which Kirsty lived. Kirsty could not open the door to him, but there was One who could, and Francis could knock!

"God help me!" he cried, as he lay on his face to live where once he had lain on his face to die. For the rising again is the sepulchre. The world itself is one vast sepulchre for the heavenly resurrection. We are all busy within the walls of our tomb burying our dead that the corruptible may perish, and the incorruptible go free.

Francis Gordon came out of that earth house a risen man. His will was born. He climbed to the spot where Kirsty and he had sat together, and there, with the vast clear heaven over his head, threw himself once more on his face and lifted up his heart to the heart from whence he came.

34 / The Neighbors

Francis had eaten nothing since the morning, and felt like one in a calm ethereal dream as he walked home to Weelset in the soft dusk of an evening that would never be night, but die into day. No one saw him enter the house. No one met him on the ancient spiral stairs as with apprehensive anticipation he made his way slowly toward the drawing room.

He had just set his foot on the little landing by its door when a wild scream came from the room. He flung the door open and darted in.

His mother rushed into his arms, enveloped from head to foot in a cone of fire. She was making a wild flight for the stairs, which would have been death to her had she reached them. Francis held her fast, but she struggled so wildly that he had to throw her on the floor before he could do anything to deliver her. Then he flung the rug over her, the tablecloth, his coat, and one of the window curtains, tearing it fiercely from the rings.

Having got the fire out, he rang the bell frantically, but had to ring it three more times, for service in that house was deadened by a frequent fury of summons. Two of the maids—there was no manservant in the house now—came and laid their mistress on a mattress and carried her to her room. Gordon's hands and arms were so severely burned that he could do nothing beyond directing the servants.

The doctor was sent for and came quickly. He examined them both, then said Mrs. Gordon's injuries would have caused him no anxiety but for her habits: their consequences might be very serious, and every possible care must be taken of her.

Disabled as he was, Francis sat by her till the morning, and the night's nursing did far more for him than for his mother. For as he saw how she suffered, and interpreted her moans by what he had felt and was still feeling in his own hands and arms, a great pity awoke in him.

What a lost life his mother's had been! Was this to be the end of it? The old kindness she had shown him in his childhood and youth, especially when he was in any bodily trouble, came back upon him, and a new love, gathering up in it all the intermittent love of days long gone by, sprang to life in his heart, and he saw that the one thing given him to do was to deliver his mother.

The task did not seem so bad as long as she continued incapable of resisting, annoying, or deceiving him. But the time speedily came when he perceived that the continuous battle rather than war of duty and inclination must be fought and in some measure won in himself before he could hope to stir up any smallest skirmish of sacred warfare in the soul of his mother. What added to the bitterness of this preliminary war was that the very nature of the contest required actions that seemed unbecoming and even disgraceful. There was no pride or pomp of glorious war in this poor, domestic strife, this seemingly sordid and unheroic, miserably unheroic, yet high, eternal contest!

But now that Francis was awake to his duty, the best of his nature awoke to meet its calls, and he drew upon a growing store of love for strength. He learned not to mind looking tyrannical, selfish, and heartless in the endeavor to be truly loving and lovingly true. He did not have Kirsty to support him, but he went to the same fountain from which Kirsty herself drew strength.

The gradually approaching strife between mother and son burst out the same moment the devilish thirst for drink awoke to its cruel tyranny. It was a mercy to them both that it reasserted itself while the mother was yet helpless. Francis was no longer afraid of her, but it was the easier because of her condition, although not the less painful for him to frustrate her desire. Neither did it make it the less painful that already her countenance, which the outward fire had not half so much disfigured as that which she had herself applied inwardly, had begun to remind him of the face he had long ago loved a little. But this only made him yet more determined that she should drink not an ounce more.

In carrying out his resolve, Francis found it especially hard to fight, along with the bad in his mother, the good in himself: the lower forms of love rose against the higher, and had to be put down. To see the scintillation of his mother's eyes at the sound of any liquid, and know how easily he could give her an hour of false happiness, tore his heart, while her fierce abuse hardly passed the portals of his brain. Her condition was so pitiful that her words could not make him angry.

She would yell that it was he who set her clothes on fire rather than her own drunkenness. Yet the worst answer he ever gave was, "Mother, you *know* you don't mean it."

"I do mean it, Francis!" she replied, glaring at him.

He stooped toward her tenderly. She struck him on the face so hard that his nose started to bleed. He went back a step, and stood looking at her sadly as he wiped it away.

"Crying!" she said. "You always were a coward, Francis!"

But the word had no more sting left for him.

"It's the doctor who's put him up to it!" said Mrs. Gordon to herself after Francis left the room. "But we shall soon be rid of him. If there's any more of this nonsense, then I shall have to shut Francis up again. That will teach him to behave better to his mother!"

When at length Mrs. Gordon was able to go about the house again, it was at once to discover that things were not to be as they had been before. Then the combat deepened. The battle of the warrior is with confused noise and garments rolled in blood, but how much harder and worthier battles are fought, not in shining armor, but amid filth and squalor—physical as well as moral— on a most wearisome and commonplace field.

It was essential to success that there should be no traitor

among the servants, and Francis took his lairdship firmly in hand and made them understand what his measures were. When he therefore one day found his mother, for the first time, under the influence of strong drink, he summoned them and told them that he would part with the whole household of them before he would fail to achieve his end if no one revealed how the thing had come about. Thereupon the youngest, a mere girl, burst into tears and confessed that she had bought the whiskey for her. Francis hardly thought it possible his mother should have money in her possession, so careful was he to prevent it. He questioned the young servant further and found that she had provided the half crown required, and that her mistress had given her in return a valuable brooch, an heirloom, which was hers only to wear, not to give. He took this from her, repaid the half crown, gave her wages up to the next term, and sent her home immediately with Mrs. Bremner. Her father being one of his own tenants, Francis rode to his place the next morning, laid before him the whole matter, and advised him to keep the girl at home for a year or two, at which time he would try her again in the house.

This one evil success gave such a stimulus to Mrs. Gordon's passion that her rage, which had been abating a little, blazed up at once as fierce as at first. But, miserable as the whole thing was, and trying as he found the necessary watchfulness, Gordon held out bravely. At the end of six months, however, during which time no fresh indulgence of her thirst had been possible to his mother, he had hardly gained the least ground for hoping that any poorest waking of a desire toward betterment had taken place in her.

All this time he had not once been to Corbyknowe. He had nevertheless been seeing David Barclay three or four times a week. He had told David how he stood with Kirsty, and how, while refusing him, she had shown him his duty to his mother. He told him also that he was now seeing things with different eyes and was trying to do what was right. But he dared not speak to Kirsty on the subject lest she should think that he was doing it merely for her sake, as she would, after what had passed between them, be well justified in thinking. As no man of business, he asked David, as his father's friend and his own, to look into his affairs, and, so far as his other duties would permit, to begin to place things on at least a better footing.

To this request David had at once gladly consented.

David found everything connected with the property in a sad condition. The agent who handled Weelset's financial affairs, although honest, was weak and had so given way to Mrs. Gordon that much havoc had been made and much money wasted. He was now in bad health, and had lost all heart for his work. But the agent had turned nothing to his own advantage and was quite ready, under David's supervision, to do his best for the restoration of order and the curtailing of expenses.

All that David saw in the next few months in his interaction with the young laird convinced him that he was on the high road of becoming a man of genuine conscience, that the foolishness of his youth had at last been put behind him, and that the manly strengths of his father were at last asserting themselves, as David himself had long hoped and prayed they would. He reported at home what he saw, and said what he believed, and his wife and daughter plainly perceived that his heart was lighter than it had been for many a day. Kirsty listened, said little, asked a question here and there, and thanked God. For her father brought her not only the good news that Francis was doing his best for his mother but that he had begun to open his eyes to the fact that he had his own part in the well-being of all on his land; that the property was not his for the filling of his pockets, or for the carrying out of schemes of his own, but for the general and individual comfort and progress. His eyes began to look around him for what he might do for his tenants, for his servants, and for ways he might turn Weelset into a source of prosperity and pride for all who were connected with it, rather than a source of embarrassment and financial drain.

Mrs. Gordon's temper seemed for a time to have changed

from fierce to sullen, but by degrees she began to show herself not altogether indifferent to the continuous attentions of her inexorable son. It is true she received them as her right, but he yielded her a right immeasurably beyond that she would have claimed. He would play cribbage with her for hours at a time, and every day for months read to her as long as she would listen—from Scott and Dickens and Wilkie Collins and Charles Reade.

One day, after much pleading, she agreed to go out for a drive with him. When round the door came a beautiful new carriage and such a pair of horses as she had never seen, she could not help expressing satisfaction. Francis told her they were at her command, but if ever she took unfair advantage of them, he would send both carriage and horses away.

She was furious at his daring to speak so to *her*, and almost returned to her room, but thought better of it and went with him. She did not, however, speak a word to him the whole way. The next morning he let her go alone. After that he sometimes went with her, and sometimes not: the desire of his heart was to help her become a free woman.

She was quite steady for a while, and her spirits began to return. The hopes of her son rose high, and he almost ceased to fear.

35 / Kirsty Gives Advice Again _____

It was again midsummer, and just a year since they parted on the Horn.

One day Francis appeared at Corbyknowe and found Kirsty in the kitchen. She received him as if nothing had ever come between them, but at once noted that he was in trouble. She proposed that they should go out together.

It was a long way to be silent, but they walked and walked, and at last came to the spot from which they started for the race earlier recorded before either of them said a word.

"Will you not sit down, Kirsty?" said Francis at length.

For answer she dropped on the same stone where she was sitting when she challenged him, and Francis took his seat on its neighbor.

"I've had a sore time of it since you showed me how little I was worth your notice, Kirsty," he began.

"Ay," returned Kirsty, "but every hoor o' it has shown what the real Francie was."

"I don't know, Kirsty. All I can say is that I don't think nearly so much of myself as I did then."

"And I think a heap more o' ye," answered Kirsty. "I canna but think ye're upon the right road noo, Francie."

"I hope I am, but I'm aye finding out something more in me that will never do."

"And ye'll keep findin' that oot sae long as there's anythin' left but what's like himsel'."

"I understand you, Kirsty. But I came to you today not to say

202

anything about myself but just because I couldn't do without your help. I wouldn't have presumed but that I thought, although I don't deserve it, for old kindness you might say what you would advise."

"I'll do that, Francie—no for auld kindness but for kindness never auld. What's wrong wi' ye?"

"It's my mother . . . she's broken out again!"

"I dinna wonder. I hae heard o' such things."

"It's just taken the hope out of me. What *am* I to do?"

"Ye canna do better than ye hae been doin'. Jist begin again."

"I bought her a bonny carriage, with as fine a pair as you ever saw, as I daresay your father has told you. And they weren't lost upon her, for she always had a keen eye for a horse. And up till yesterday, all went well, till I was thinking I could trust her anywhere. But in the afternoon, as she was out for a drive, one of the horses broke a shoe, and thinking nothing of the risk to a human soul, but only of the risk to the poor horse, the fool driver stopped at a smithy no farther than the next door from a public house, and took the horse into the smithy, leaving the smith's lad at the head of the other horse. So what should my mother do but get out on the other side of the carriage and walk straight into the public house! Whether she took anything there I don't know, but she must have brought a bottle home with her, for this morning she was drunk—as foul drunk as you ever saw a man in the marketplace."

He broke down and began to weep.

"And what did ye do?" asked Kirsty.

"I said nothing. I just went to the coachman and made him hitch the horses up and take his dinner with him, and mount the box and drive straight to Aberdeen, and leave the carriage where I bought it, and do the same with the horses, and come home by the coach."

As he ended the sad tale, he glanced up at Kirsty, and saw her regarding him with a look such as he had never seen, imagined, or dreamed of before. It lasted but a moment. Then her eyes dropped, and she went on with her knitting, which, as in the old days, she had brought with her.

"Now, Kirsty, what am I to do next?"

"Hae ye naethin' in yer ain mind?" she asked.

"Nothing."

"Weel, let's gae home," she returned, rising. "Maybe as we go, we'll get light upon it."

They walked in silence. Now and then Francis would look up in Kirsty's face to see if anything was coming, but saw only that she was sunk in thought. He knew she would speak the moment she had what she thought worth saying. In the meantime, he would not hurry her.

Kirsty found herself continuing to think about Mrs. Barclay in relation to horses. After some while she spoke.

"Francie," she said, "I hae thought o' somethin'. My father has aye said that yer mither was a better than ordinary good rider in her yoong days, and this is what it occurs to me to do. Gae oot and buy her the best lookin', best tempered, handiest, and easiest gaein' lady's horse ye can find. And then ye must ride wi' her wherever she goes."

"I'll do it, Kirsty. I can't go immediately, though. I'm afraid she still has whiskey left, and there's no saying what she might do before I got back. I must go home first."

"I'm no so sure that's best. Ye canna weel go and search all the chests and cupboards in the hoose she calls her own. That would anger her terrible. Nor can ye keep her frae drink by force. It seems to me that ye must take the risk o' her bottle. It mightna be an ill thing that she should disgrace hersel' oot and oot. And then ye can bring the horse back wi' ye as a fresh beginnin', like a new order o' things, and that way ye'd avoid words wi' her."

That same morning when Mrs. Gordon came to herself, she thought to behave as if nothing had happened, and rang the bell to order the carriage. The maid informed her that the coachman had driven away with it, and had not said where he was going.

"Driven away with it!" cried her mistress, jumping to her feet. "I gave him no orders!"

"I saw the laird givin' him directions, mem," rejoined the maid.

Mrs. Gordon sat down again. She began to remember what her son had said when first he gave her the carriage.

"Where did he send him?" she asked.

"I dinna ken, mem."

"Go and ask the laird to step this way."

"Please, mem, he's no in the hoose. I ken, for I saw him go—hoors ago."

"Did he go in the carriage?"

"No, mem. He gaed upon his ain feet."

"Perhaps he's come home by this time."

"I dinna think so, mem."

Mrs. Gordon went to her room, all but finished the bottle of whiskey, and threw herself on her bed. There she remained the rest of the day and night. Toward morning she woke with aching head and miserable mind. Now dozing, now tossing about in wretchedness, she lay till the afternoon. No one came near her, and she wanted no one.

At length, dizzy and despairing, her head in torture and her heart sick, she managed to get out of bed, and, unable to walk, literally crawled to the cupboard in which she had put away the precious bottle:—joy! there was a glass yet in it!

With the mouth of it to her lips, she was tilting it up to drain the last drop when the voice of her son came cheerily from the driveway that her window looked out onto.

"See what I've brought you, Mother!" he called.

Fear came upon her. She took the bottle from her mouth and put it back again in the cupboard, and crept back to her bed, her brain like a hive buzzing with devils.

When Francis entered the house, he was not surprised to learn that she had not left her room. He did not try to see her.

The next morning she felt a little better, and had some tea and toast. Still she did not care to get up. She shrank from meeting her son, and the abler she grew to think, the more unwilling she was to see him. He came to her room, but she heard him coming, turned her head the other way, and pretended to be asleep. Again and again, almost involuntarily, she half rose, remembering the last of the whiskey, but as often lay down again, loathing the cause of her headache.

Stronger and stronger grew her unwillingness to face her son: she had so thoroughly proved herself unfit to be trusted. She began to feel toward him as she had sometimes felt toward her mother when she had been naughty. She began to see that she could make her peace, with him or with herself, only by acknowledging her weakness. Aided by her misery, she had begun to perceive that she could not trust herself. She had resented the idea that she could not keep herself from drink if she pleased, for she knew she could. But she had not pleased. How could she ever ask him to trust her again?

What further passed in her I cannot tell. Mrs. Gordon began gradually to realize that the only thing that was then helping her was the strong hand of her son upon her. But there was another help that is never lacking where it can find an entrance; and now for the first time she began tentatively to pray, "Lead me not into temptation."

Undoubtedly, during all the period of her excesses, the soul of the woman in her better moments had been ashamed to know her for the thing she was. It could not, when she was at her worse, go along with her idea of a lady, poor as that idea was, to drink whiskey till she did not know what she did next. And when the sleeping woman God made wakes up to see in what a house she lives, she will soon grasp broom and bucket, and not cease her cleansing while there is so much as a spot left on wall or ceiling or floor.

How the waking comes, who can tell? God knows what he wants us to do, and what we can do, and how to help us. What I have to tell is that the next morning, Mrs. Gordon came down to breakfast, and finding her son already seated at the table, came up behind him, without a word set the bottle with the last glass of whiskey in it before him, went to her place at the table, gave him one sorrowful look, and sat down.

His heart understood and rejoiced.

Neither spoke until breakfast was almost over. Then Francis said, "You've grown so much younger, Mother, it is quite time you took to riding again! I've been out to buy a horse for you. Remembering the sort of pony you bought for me, I thought I should like to see whether I could please you with a horse of my buying."

"Silly boy!" she returned with a rather pitiful laugh. "Do you suppose at my age I am going to make a fool of myself on horseback? You forget how old I am."

"Not a bit of it, Mother! If ever you rode as David Barclay says you did, I don't see why you shouldn't ride still. He's a splendid creature! David told me you liked a big fellow. Just put on your riding clothes, and we'll have a gallop across the field and astonish the old man a bit!"

"My dear boy, I have no nerve left for that sort of thing. I'm not the woman I was. It's my own fault I know, and I'm both sorry and ashamed."

"We are both going to try harder to be good, Mother," said Francis.

The poor woman pressed her handkerchief with both hands to her face, wept for a few moments, then rose and left the room. In an hour she was ready and out looking for Francis. Her riding habit was a little too tight for her, but wearable enough. The horses were sent for, and they mounted.

36 / The Ride

There was at Corbyknowe a young, well-bred horse that David had reared himself. Kirsty had been teaching him to carry a lady.

That same morning Kirsty had put on a blue riding habit that Lady Macintosh had given her, and was out on the highest slope of the farm, hoping to catch a sight of the two Gordons on horseback together. She had been out about an hour when she saw them coming along between the castle and Corbyknowe. She went straight for a certain point in the road so as to reach it simultaneously with them.

"Who can that be?" said Mrs. Gordon as they trotted gently along. "She rides well! But she seems to be alone! Is there nobody with her?"

As she spoke the young horse came flying over a dry-stane-dyke in fine style.

"Why she's an accomplished horsewoman!" exclaimed Mrs. Gordon. "She must be a stranger! There's not a lady within thirty miles of Weelset who can ride like that!"

"No such stranger as you think, Mother," rejoined Francis. "That's Kirsty Barclay of Corbyknowe."

"How could it be, Francis! The girl rides like a lady!"

Francis smiled, perhaps a little triumphantly. Something like what lay in the smile the mother read in it, for it roused at once both her jealousy and her pride. *Her* son to fall in love with a girl that was not even a lady! A Gordon of Weelset to marry a tenant's daughter! Impossible!

Kirsty was now in the road before them, riding slowly in the same direction. It was the progress, however, not the horse that was slow: his frolics, especially when the other horse drew near, kept his rider sufficiently occupied.

Mrs. Gordon quickened her pace and passed without turning her head or looking at her, but so close and with so sudden a rush that Kirsty's horse half wheeled, and bounded over the dyke by the roadside. Her rudeness annoyed her son, and he jumped his horse into the field and joined Kirsty, letting his mother ride on, and contenting himself with keeping her in sight. After a few moments' talk, however, he suggested that they should overtake her. They cut off a great loop of the road through the field, passed her at great speed, then turned and met her. She had by this time got over her little temper and was prepared to behave with propriety.

"What a lovely horse you have, Miss Barclay!" she said, without any other greeting. "How much do you want for him?"

"He is but half broken," answered Kirsty, "or I would offer to trade with you. From the look of yours, I almost wonder that you would talk of wanting another."

"He is a beauty—is he not?" replied Mrs. Gordon. "This is my first trial of him. Francis gave me him only this morning. He is as quiet as a lamb."

"There, Donal," said Kirsty to her horse, "take an example by yer betters. Jist look at hoo he stands!—The laird has a true eye for a horse, ma'am," she went on, "but he always says he inherited it from you."

Mrs. Gordon said nothing, but looked kindly at her son.

"How did you learn to ride so well, Kirsty?" she asked.

"I suppose I got it from my father, ma'am. I began with the cows."

"Ah, how is old David?" returned Mrs. Gordon. "I have seen him once or twice about the castle lately, but have not spoken to him."

"He is very well, thank you. Will you not come up to the Knowe and rest for a moment? My mother would be very happy to see you."

"Not today, Kirsty. I haven't been on horseback for years and am already tired. We shall turn for home here. Good morning."

"Good morning, ma'am. Goodbye, Mr. Gordon!" said Kirsty cheerfully, wheeling her horse to set him straight at a steep grassy brae.

The laird and his mother sat and looked at Kirsty as her horse tore up the slope.

"She can ride—can't she, Mother?" said Francis.

"Well enough for a tomboy," answered Mrs. Gordon.

"She rides to please her horse now, but she'll have him as quiet as yours before long," rejoined her son, both a little angry and a little amused at Kirsty being called a tomboy when she had grown in his heart to be an angel.

"Yes," resumed his mother, as if she was determined to be fair, "she does ride well. If only she were a lady so I might ask her to ride with me. After all, it's none of my business what she is—so long as you don't want to marry her!" she concluded with an attempt at a laugh.

"But I do want to marry her, Mother!" rejoined Francis.

A short year before, his mother would have said what immediately sprang to her mind, and it would not have been pleasant to hear. But now she was afraid of her son, and was silent. To be dethroned in castle Weelset by the daughter of one of her own lowly tenants, for as such she thought of them, was indeed galling. *The impudent lassie!* she thought; *she's ridden on her horse into the heart of the laird!* But she calmed herself before she spoke.

"You might have any lady in the land!" she said at length.

"If I could, Mother, it would be just as vain to try to find Kirsty's equal anywhere."

"You might at least have shown your mother the respect of choosing a lady to sit in her place! You drive me from the house!"

"Mother," said Francis, "I have twice asked Kirsty Barclay to be my wife, and she has twice refused me."

"Surely you don't plan to try her again! She had her reasons!

No doubt she never meant to let you slip, but it's done now, good riddance, and now you are free from her."

"I don't want to be free from her."

"Good heavens! What are you saying?"

"You're right, Mother, she had her reasons. And now that I understand them, I love and respect her all the more for what she did to me. She made me face myself as I was. She never did like all the others, who pretended I was a fine fellow when I wasn't. She spoke the truth about me to my face. In that she showed me more love than anyone else ever has in my life. I owe her everything of what I have become."

"More than your own mother! Surely you can't—how can you say—!"

"Mother, you compel me!" he said. "When I came home ill, and, as I thought, dying, you called me bad names and drove me from the house. Kirsty found me in a hole in the earth—by then I *was* actually dying—and saved my life."

"Good heavens, Francis! Are you mad still? How dare you tell such horrible falsehoods of your own mother? You never came near me! You went straight to Corbyknowe."

"Ask Mrs. Bremner if I speak the truth. She ran out after me but could not catch up with me. You drove me out, and if you do not know it now, you do not need to be told how it is that you have forgotten it."

She knew what he meant and was silent.

"When I came home, she rescued my physical body, then helped open my spiritual eyes as well. Before, she had loved me by rejecting my foolishness and pride; now, she loved me by nursing me back to health and helping me believe in myself again, and in the bonny man, as she and Steenie call him. Her ministration brought me to my right mind. If it were not for Kirsty, I should be in my grave or wandering the earth as a maniac. Even alive and well as I am, I should not be with you now, trying in small measure to minister to your need as she did mine, had she not shown me my plain duty before God."

"I thought as much! All this tyranny of yours, all your insolence lately to your mother, comes from the power of that lowborn woman over you!"

"Lowborn, Mother? Her father was your husband's dearest friend."

"I declare to you, Francis Gordon, if you marry her, I will leave the house."

He made her no answer, and they rode the rest of the way in silence. But in that silence things grew clearer to him. Why should he take pains to persuade his mother to a consent that she had no right to withhold. His desire was altogether reasonable: why should its fulfillment depend on the unreason of one who had not even the strength to order her own behavior? He had to help God save her, not please her, gladly as he would have done both.

When he had helped her from the saddle, he would have remounted and ridden at once to Corbyknowe, but was afraid to leave her. She shut herself in her room till she could bear her own company no longer, and then went to the drawing room, where Francis read to her and played several games of backgammon with her. Soon after dinner she retired, saying the ride had wearied her.

The moment Francis knew she was in bed, he got his horse and galloped to the Knowe.

37 / The Horn Again

When he arrived, there was no light in the house: all had gone to bed.

Not wanting to disturb the father and mother, he rode quietly to the back of the house where Kirsty's room looked out on the garden. He called her softly. In a moment she peeped out, then opened her window.

"Could ye come doon a minute, Kirsty?" said Francis.

"I'll be wi' ye in less than that," she replied. He had hardly more than dismounted when she was by his side.

He told her what had passed between him and his mother since she left them, including what he had told her of his intentions.

"It's a real bonny night," said Kirsty, "and we'll jist take oor time to turn the thing over—that is, if ye arena too tired, Francie."

"Na, ha!" he replied.

"Come," she said. "We'll put the beastie up first."

She led the horse into the dark stable, took his bridle off, put a halter on him, slackened his girths, and gave him a feed of corn—all in the dark. That done, she and Francis set out for the Horn.

The whole night seemed to be thinking of the day that was gone. All doing seemed at an end; yea, God himself seemed to be resting and thinking. The peace of it sank into their hearts and filled them so that they walked a long way without speaking. There was no wind, and only the pale light of the dying day behind, and the rising day to come—the light one in the same;

the stars overhead were bright. The air was like the clear dark inside some diamonds. The only sound that broke the stillness was the voice of Kirsty, sweet and low—and it was as if the dim starry vault thought, rather than she uttered, the words she quoted:

> Summer Night, come from God,
> On your beauty, I see,
> A still wave has flowed
> Of Eternity.

At a certain spot on the ridge of the Horn, Francis stopped.

"This is whaur ye left me this time last year, Kirsty," he said; "—left me wi' my Maker to make a man o' me. And noo I can tell ye wi' all my heart—thank ye for lovin' me as ye did! Thank ye for lovin' me enough to make me face my ain miserable self! There arena many wi' sich a kind o' love for their brithers and sisters, Kirsty! But I'm thankful to God that ye're one o' the best o' them!"

Kirsty sighed in contentment. The peace in her heart came not from hearing such words spoken about herself, but rather from the change in the man she had loved since very childhood.

There was a low stone just visible among the heather; she seated herself upon it. Francis threw himself among the heather and lay looking up in her face.

"'Tis the kind o' night," said Kirsty, "that I always imagined the sort when Steenie fancied the bonny man was aye gaein' aboot here on the Horn."

"Ay, Steenie was sich a one o' God's creatures. I only wish I'd had the good sense to see him as ye saw him yersel' when I was yoonger."

"Sometimes I think, Francie, that he and his bonny man come walkin' here together noo."

"Do ye fancy him talkin' to ye like?"

"Na, na. I doobt there's talkin' frae beyond the grave. The bonny man himsel' said there's nae reason for it. There's many a Scot wi' the second sight, but I think that's wi' the heart only, no wi' the eyes and ears."

They were silent a minute, both thinking of Steenie. Kirsty was the first to speak again.

"That mother o' yers is almost ower muckle for ye, Francie," she said.

"It's no that often, Kirsty, that ye tell me what I ken already."

"Well, Francie, then tell me somethin' I don't ken aboot. I would like to hear hoo ye won through wi' her since that day we parted here last year."

Without a moment's hesitation, Francis began the tale—telling all about his own inner struggles, the opening of his eyes toward himself and toward his Father above, and then how he had tried to serve his mother and the results. He made plain to Kirsty that there was much in what took place that he did not understand.

When he ended, Kirsty rose and said, "Would ye please sit upon that stone, Francie?"

In pure obedience he rose from the heather and sat on the stone.

She went behind him and clasped his head round the temples with her shapely, strong, faithful hands.

"I ken ye noo for a man, Francis Gordon. Ye hae set yersel' to do *his* will, and no yer own, to serve another, no yersel'. For that, ye're a child o' the King, and a king yersel', and for want of a better crown, I crown ye wi' my own two hands."

Then she came round in front of him, he sitting almost as one bewildered, and taking no part in the solemn ceremony except that of submission.

"And ye willna be angert wi' me, Kirsty," he said, "for comin' to ye a third time—though the first as a man—to ask ye to be my wife?"

For answer, Kirsty knelt slowly down before him, laying her head on his knees, and saying, "To follow yer crownin', here's yer kingdom, Francis—my head and my heart! Do wi' me what ye will. I'm ready to be yers at last."

"Come home wi' me," he answered in a voice choked with emotion. "Come and share the castle wi' me, and help me save my mother."

"I will," she said. Then they rose and went.

They had gone about halfway to the farm before either spoke. Then Kirsty said, "Francie, there's jist one thing I must beg o' ye—that ye winna make me take the head o' yer table. I canna but think it an ungracious thing that a young woman like me, the son's wife, should put the man's own mither, his father's wife, out o' the place whaur his father set her. I want to come as her daughter, no as mistress o' the hoose in her place. Promise me that, Francie, and I'll soon take the most part o' the trouble o' her off yer hands."

"Ye're aye right, Kirsty," answered Francis. "As ye wish."

38 / Kirsty's Song

The next morning, Kirsty told her parents that she was going to marry Francie.

"Ye do right, my bairn," said her father. "He's come in sight o' his high callin', and I must say I'm finally able to hold up my head in pride at the memory o' his father. I had begun wonderin' what I would say to my auld friend when we met, me havin' done his son sae little good. But noo I can see it's no possible for ye longer to refuse him. He's a good lad, and on the way to bein' better."

"But eh, what am I to do wi'oot ye, Kirsty," moaned her mother.

"Ye remember, Mother," answered Kirsty, "hoo I would be oot all the long day wi' Steenie, and then ye never thought ye didna hae me."

"Na, never. I aye kenned I had the two o' ye."

"Weel, it's no God's innocent but a devil's gowk I'll hae to look after noo, and I'll hae to come home every possible chance to get heartenin' frae you and my father, or I winna be able to bide it. Eh, Mother, after Steenie, it'll be sore tryin' to spend the day wi' *her*! It's no that she'll ever be full: I'll see to that! It's that she'll aye be empty, aye ringin' wi emptiness!"

Here Kirsty turned to her father, and said, "Will ye give me a dowry, Father?"

"Ay, will I, lassie—what ye like, sae far as I hae it to give."

"Donal, the horse—that's a'. I'll hae to ride wi' Francie's

217

mother, and I would like to hae somethin' beneath me that ye
gave me. The creature'll aye hang toward the Knowe, and, when
I give him his will, he'll bring me back home to ye by himsel'.''

Kirsty and Francis were married four months later. He had
just turned twenty-five, she would do so in another month or two.
They had these advantages that many young lovers do not: they
had known one another many years, knew the best and the worst
about each other, were not starry-eyed, and most importantly, had
been the best of friends before they had been lovers. Kirsty had
been in no hurry to fall in love. They had played together as
children, enjoyed each other as youths, learned to respect one
another as young man and young woman. Thus their marriage
was built on the firm foundation of time, deepened by maturity.
When love came, therefore, they were old enough to begin to
understand a little of what it was.

Mrs. Gordon now manages the house, and her reward is to
sit at the head of the table. But she pays Kirsty infinitely more
for the privilege than any but Kirsty can know, in the form of
leisure for things she likes far better than housekeeping. Now that
Mrs. Gordon's temptation to drink is altogether gone, the laird
and Kirsty—she refuses to be called *Lady* Gordon—ride often
about their land, visiting their tenants to see what they might do
for them.

Francis is greatly beloved by his people, and reminds not a
few old enough to remember of his father. They say he is sure to
be in straits within a year from the low rents he charges. But
Francis is not anxious; he knows from whence comes his provi-
sion.

Francis offered his father-in-law the position of factor to the
estate, but David declined. He said he and his Marion would
content themselves to remain at Corbyknowe for the rest of their
days. David is now approaching sixty-nine years, still strong, still
erect, and still a favorite in the neighborhood. His hair is still

gray, though thinner. Kirsty visits her mother and father almost every day or two.

Kirsty is unchanged. As for Francis, the changes wrought in him are not visible on the surface. The only indication one might gather that he is indeed a different man would come from observing him on a summer's evening, walking upon the Horn. No longer are his eyes and ears and other senses earthbound. No longer does the heather brush past his feet, does the wind blow softly on his face, does the earthy aroma of peat fill his nostrils, and go past him without notice. Now the heather, the wind, and the peat *speak* to him. And this tells volumes about the sort of man he has become.

Sometimes he and Kirsty go out onto the Horn in an evening, he with a pencil and pad, she with a heart full of poetry and song. This is one of the songs which came to Kirsty recently, and which her husband wrote down:

LOVE IS HOME

> Love is the part, and love is the whole;
> Love is the robe, and love is the pall;
> Ruler of heart and brain and soul,
> Love is the lord and the slave of all!
> I thank thee, Love, that thou lov'st me;
> I thank thee more that I love thee.
> Love is the rain, and love is the air;
> Love is the earth that holdeth fast;
> Love is the root that is buried there,
> Love is the open flower at last!
> I thank thee, Love all round about,
> That the eyes of my love are looking out.
> Love is the sun and love is the sea;
> Love is the tide that comes and goes;
> Flowing and flowing it comes to me;
> Ebbing and ebbing to thee it flows!
> Oh, my sun, and my wind, and tide!
> My sea, and my shore, and all beside!
> Light, oh light that art by showing;
> Wind, oh wind that liv'st by motion;

Thought, oh thought that art by knowing;
Will that art born in self-devotion!
Love is you, though not all of you know it;
Ye are not love, yet ye always show it!
Faithful creator, heart-longed-for father,
Home of our heart-infolded brother,
Home to thee all thy glories gather—
All are thy love, and there is no other!
O Love-at-rest; we loves that roam—
Home unto thee, we are coming home!

But more often than not, they go walking on the Horn with
nothing but each other, hand in hand, listening for the voice of
the bonny man.